D0736110

THE CONTAMINATED CASE OF THE

COOKING CONTEST

This book is a work of fiction. Names, characters, businesses, organizations, places, events and incidents are either the product of the author's imagination or, in the case of historical events or persons, used fictitiously. Any resemblance to actual events or persons, living or dead, is likewise intended fictitiously.

Copyright © 2015 Peter Wong and Pendred Noyce

All rights reserved. No part of this book may be used or reproduced, stored in a retrieval system, or transmitted by any means - electronic, mechanical, photocopying, recording or in any manner whatsoever without written permission from the publisher except in the case of brief quotations embodied in critical articles and reviews.

For further information, contact:
Tumblehome Learning, Inc.
P.O. Box 171386
Boston, MA 02117
http://www.tumblehomelearning.com

Library of Congress Control Number: 2015937050

Wong, Peter / Noyce, Pendred
The Contaminated Case of the Cooking Contest /
Peter Wong and Pendred Noyce - 1st ed

ISBN 978-0-9907829-2-6

1. Children - Fiction 2. Science Fiction 3. Mystery

Illustrations: Yu-Yu Chin (金祐羽)
Cover Art: Yu-Yu Chin (金祐羽)
Cover design: mighty media®

Printed in Taiwan

10 9 8 7 6 5 4 3 2 1

THE CONTAMINATED CASE OF THE

COOKING CONTEST

By Peter Wong & Pendred Noyce

Illustrated by Yu-Yu Chin

Copyright 2015, All rights reserved.

Tumblehome learning

Table of Content

Cruise Ship Schematic

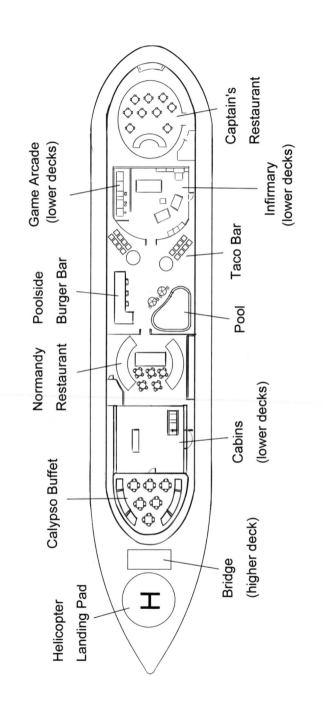

Helicopter
Landing Pad

Calypso Buffet

Normandy
Restaurant

Poolside
Burger Bar

Game Arcade
(lower decks)

Bridge
(higher deck)

Cabins
(lower decks)

Pool

Taco Bar

Infirmary
(lower decks)

Captain's
Restaurant

Chapter 1

Cruise Ship Departs Miami

Saturday

Clinton Chang stood next to his friend Mae Harris on the deck of the giant cruise ship, waving good-bye to all the people on shore even though he didn't know any of them. "I can't believe we're really going on a cruise," he said. "I can't believe your mom let you bring me along."

Mae's mother was a nurse, and she would be working in the ship infirmary, the medical center, in return for a free cruise and small cabin for three. Clinton added, "I hope nobody on this cruise gets sick, so your mom has lots of time to just relax and have fun."

"I just hope I don't get seasick," Mae Harris said. "You know me and motion sickness."

1

"Don't even think about it," said Clinton. He nudged Mae with an elbow. "You know you have to get over that to be an astronaut. But hey, you did all right on the flight down to Miami."

Clinton knew how much Mae had been looking forward to this trip. She worked so hard at school that sometimes she got really tense. For the last couple of weeks she'd been acting crabby and nervous. He knew she'd packed and repacked her suitcase for a week, trying to foresee anything she might need. Clinton, on the other hand, just threw his stuff into a duffel bag at the last minute. The two of them were so different, he doubted they'd even be friends if not for some pretty amazing adventures they'd had with the Galactic Academy of Science.

As the ship pulled away from the wharf, Clinton turned from the rail and looked down the length of the ship. It was taller than most buildings he'd seen, and it seemed to stretch as long as a city block. "It really is like a city," he said. "A floating city."

"I know," said Mae. "Let's go back to the room and check the list of activities for today. We need to plan how to get the most out of everything."

They took the stairs down a few decks and then walked through a series of corridors to a bank of elevators. They passed the lifeboats where they had practiced the muster drill for emergencies as soon as they boarded.

"I hope we never have to use the lifeboats," Mae said.

"Don't worry," Clinton said. "I'm a strong swimmer, and I'll help you if we go overboard."

"Great," said Mae. "Wow. I feel so safe."

They took the elevator down several decks, walked past the conference rooms and purser desk where they had signed in, and descended one more staircase. Finally they reached their cabin, where Mae opened the door.

There were no windows, or portholes, as Clinton reminded himself they were called. Still, there was a double bed that Mae and her mother would share while Clinton slept on the pullout couch. It looked a little lumpy, but he didn't care.

Mae's mother was still unpacking clothes and arranging the room. "There you are," she said when they entered. "Would you like to get something to eat before I start my shift in the infirmary?"

"Ooh, food," Clinton said. "Where do we go first?" One of the cool things about this cruise was that there were supposed to be different kinds of food all over the ship.

"Let's try the buffet," Mae's mother, Gina, replied. "Make sure you wash your hands first. Actually, I'd like you to wash your hands very often while we're on the ship. Cruises are fun, but there's always the chance of a fast-spreading illness. Have you heard of norovirus?"

Mae wrinkled her nose. "Sally Hingston told me all about it when she found out I invited Clinton instead of her. Stomach aches, diarrhea, vomit splashing everywhere…"

Clinton made a face, and Mae continued, "Isn't there a vaccine or something we can take?"

Mae's mom shook her head. "There's no vaccine for norovirus. Washing your hands is your best defense. Other than that you should focus on having fun, not worrying. Now wash your hands."

As Clinton and Mae jostled for space at the small sink, Mae's mother continued from the other room, "Speaking of food, did you see the notice about the cooking contest? There are actually two cooking contests on board. One is for adults and the other for kids your age. You two should sign up."

When they came out of the bathroom, Mae's mom gave them some brochures and shooed them away. "Why don't you go find a table while I finish up here. I'll be there in a minute."

Mae and Clinton made their way to the Calypso Buffet and found a quiet corner where they could look out to sea. Mae flipped open the brochure for the kids' cooking contest and started reading the contest rules aloud. Clinton let his mind drift. "I like to eat," Clinton said. "I'll be too busy eating to cook. I heard you can eat anytime you want on the cruise ship."

Mae let the brochure drop. "You're probably right. The only thing I know about cooking is from watching a couple of cooking shows. I never cook at home, and Mom's always in too much of a hurry to make anything fancy. We'd never win."

"Wait a minute," said Clinton. "I never said we couldn't *win*."

Just then, a whooshing sound filled the air, and there in front of them, in the seat they'd been saving for Mae's mom, sat their friend from the future—Selectra Volt.

Selectra was dressed in her usual skin-tight green outfit covered with pink puffballs. Her green and pink hair stuck out in its usual cheerful way, but she was frowning.

"Whoa, Selectra," Clinton said. "How'd you find us here?"

"We try to keep track of our G.A.S. recruits," Selectra said. "You are Clinton Chang, Asian-American, been on four missions?"

"Come on, you know that," Clinton said. "Can't we do without this official stuff?"

"Selectra!" Mae interrupted. "How can you just pop in like this, in the middle of a crowded room?"

Selectra turned her head to Mae, looking unconcerned. "It's easy to escape notice in a crowd. And you are Mae Jemison Harris, African-American, and want to be an astronaut like Mae Jemison?"

"You already know that," Mae said. "Really, Selectra, you can be so annoying."

"Do we have a mission?" Clinton asked.

"Yes. No. Soon." Selectra said. She blinked. "That is, maybe. Somebody is groobing things up."

"What do you mean?" Clinton demanded.

Selectra took a big breath that made her spiky hair sway and said, "We may need you to investigate a case aboard the cruise ship. Someone here may get sick and could even die, and it's a person who, mmm…well, we can't afford to lose that person. The person is known in my time as a very important person."

"Who is it?" Mae asked.

"I can't tell you that," Selectra said. "You know the rules for the Galactic Academy of Science: First, I have to verify your identities. Second, I cannot go with you into the past where you may need to travel to solve this mission. Third and top, I cannot tell you anything about the future."

Clinton jumped up from his chair and raised his hands in the air. He said, "It's me, isn't it?" He was only half joking. Something about all these missions for the G.A.S. was beginning to convince him he really was going to be somebody. "I'm important to the future, so we have to save *me*."

"I can't tell you who the person is," Selectra said. She seemed more serious than usual. "You need to investigate the

5

mystery on the ship. Keep your eyes open. Learn what you can about cooking and food safety. Take every opportunity. That's all I can say."

"Is Dr. G messing up this ship?" Mae asked. Dr. G was the villain Selectra had told them about on their last mission. She had explained that Dr. G led a group called S.A.G. that was committed to spreading false scientific information and computer hacking to interfere with scientific progress.

Selectra said, "We don't know if Dr. G is behind this. We don't even know if this is bad luck or an evil plot. All we know is you need to solve it." She rubbed her hand through her spiky hair and pulled an object that looked like a smart phone from her belt. "Here's your X-PA."

She laid the X-PA on the table, and Clinton picked it up. It still amazed him that a tool so small and light could be so powerful. On four occasions already, it had allowed Mae and him to travel through time and space to meet famous scientists and engineers. Its only weakness was that it ran out of power quickly at any one time and location, so they had to keep focused and work quickly.

Selectra talked in a rush, giving the standard instructions. "Your X-PA is set with the candidates to interview, various people for you to visit. Be sure to watch the Site Energy Bar so you have enough power to leave each place. You don't want to get stuck in the past. Visit the candidates and check back with the ship to see how things are going."

Clinton began to scroll through the list of "Candidates for Interview." He heard Selectra say, "Be careful. It would be totally unzwiffy for the two of you to get sick. Be careful of what you eat." By the time Clinton looked up, Selectra was gone.

"Oh, man," said Mae, wrinkling her brow. "I thought this was going to be a vacation."

"What are you talking about?" Clinton asked. "What could be more awesome? Another mission!"

"Someone's going to get really sick," Mae said. "That's going to be bad for my mom. Look, here she comes."

Mae's mother crossed the dining room and took the seat Selectra had just left. "What are you two looking so serious about?"

"The cooking contest," Clinton said. "We're thinking about the competition. I bet some of these other kids have practiced and everything."

"Wait," Mae said. "I thought you didn't want to bother with the cooking contest."

"That was before," Clinton said. "Now I want to learn all I can about cooking and food. We're going to dominate the contest. But first—we're going to dominate lunch."

Chapter 2

Nicholas Appert and Bottled Food

Paris, France, 1812, Saturday

The buffet had amazing foods on display, from fresh Belgian waffles to southern fried chicken to makimono rolls. Mae tried out some steamed dumplings, salads with whole grains, and a soup with fresh herbs. Mae's mom had a salad with steak and some freshly baked bread. As for Clinton, Mae noticed he came back twice with his plate piled high.

After lunch, when Mae's mom left for her shift at the infirmary, Mae leaned across the table to whisper to Clinton. "Which shall we do first? Visit one of the Candidates for Interview, or work on our cooking skills for the contest?"

"No way!" said Clinton. "We still have a whole ship to explore. Let's start with the game arcade."

That was so like Clinton, Mae thought, as she followed him through the crowds leaving the dining room. He was always slacking off and procrastinating when there was work to do. The arcade was dark and beeping and packed with kids. Clinton got in line for a race car driving game, but Mae went to stand near the ship's rail so she could look out over the ocean. She loved seeing the horizon where the sea met the sky without a hint of land. If she kept her eyes on the view it was almost as if she were an explorer in the distant past. Maybe this was what it would feel like to be a Mars colonist—although there she would see nothing but barren reddish rocks instead of miles of rippling water. Mae shivered at the thought, but she still yearned to be one of the first people to live on Mars.

Watching the water slide along the side of the ship, Mae had an uncomfortable thought. When they used the X-PA for time travel missions to the past, the X-PA always brought them home when they finished. But what if this time the X-PA returned them back to where they started—and the ship had moved on? She and Clinton might be left treading water in an open ocean until they drowned.

The thought bothered Mae so much that she went looking for Clinton. She found him playing air hockey with two kids around their own age, a brother and sister, both Asian-looking with a hint of something else, with shiny black hair and brown eyes. The girl lunged over her end of the table like a pouncing cat and sent the puck slamming into the goal at Clinton's end.

"Ouch," said Clinton. "You win." He waved at Mae. "Hi. I made some new friends. Mae, this is Mattias Vargas and his sister, Riley. Mattias is nice but Riley's a killer. It's their first cruise too."

Mattias rather formally shook Mae's hand, while Riley waved and then looked at her feet without saying anything. For such a fierce air hockey player, she seemed shy.

"Let's explore the rest of the ship," Mattias said.

The four of them agreed, and before long they found a climbing wall. Riley jumped onto it and scampered to the top while the others worked their way up only a couple of handholds. When Riley came down, they located a wave surfing machine, a carousel, and a whole slew of different restaurants – tacos, pizzas, fancy French, even Chinese food. They talked about foods they loved and especially those they hated, from lima beans to liver to coconut to broccoli.

Just when Mae was beginning to feel really guilty about ignoring Selectra's assignment, Riley said, "Mattias, we really need to go."

"Wait, are your parents expecting you somewhere?" Clinton asked.

Mattias shook his head. "No, it's a sort of job—more like some special homework—it's just this thing we have to do." Riley kicked his foot, and Mattias sealed his lips and nodded, smiling, as if he'd just given a speech and people were clapping.

"See you later," Riley said, and the two of them slipped away.

Clinton turned away from the departing pair and clapped his hands together just the way their teacher did when it was time for a new topic. "Right," said Clinton. "Time for our first trip, wouldn't you say?"

"Erm," May said. "Uh, that is, what if the X-PA brings us back to where the ship was when we left it instead of where it is when we come back?"

"Yikes," Clinton said. "No, I'm sure it wouldn't do that."

"How can you be sure?" Mae asked.

"Well, Selectra's careful. She cares about us. She would never…" Clinton's voice trailed off, and Mae knew he was thinking about times when Selectra had made some scary mistakes. She was a great guide, but she was also a little careless, and they knew she'd only recently made her way back off of probation.

Then Clinton perked up. "Don't worry. Time travel is instantaneous. We'll come back the moment we left. The ship won't have moved anywhere at all."

Mae let out her breath. "You're right. Stupid me. I scared myself there."

Clinton shook his head. "That was a scary thought. Now, who do we visit?" He pulled out the X-PA, and Mae looked over his shoulder as he scrolled through the names. "John Snow. Brr, sounds too cold. How about this one, in Paris? Nicolas Appert. Mmm, Paris, French food. Let's try there."

Mae stood close to Clinton as he waved the X-PA in a figure eight around them and then pushed the button. Immediately a spinning sensation took hold of her, and she seemed to see the ship shrinking away on the ocean below. She closed her eyes.

When Mae stopped spinning, she breathed in the scent of someone cooking soup. Clinton's voice said, "French, French, where is the button?"

She opened her eyes and saw a man with his back to them leaning over a large, steaming pot. He wore a soft cloth hat and a long coat in spite of the steamy heat of the room. At his elbow stood a row of jars made of dark glass.

"Excuse me," Mae said, except that the X-PA made the words come out *Pardonnez-moi.*

The man turned and looked them up and down. His thin nose twitched. "What do you want?"

"Ah, *monsieur*, we are looking for Nicolas Appert," Clinton said. "We want to learn about his method of preserving food."

"Is the Emperor Bonaparte sending children to inspect my invention? I am Appert. Do you want to see how I won the prize money?" the man asked.

"We weren't sent by anyone," Mae said. "We're just curious about what you're doing with these foods. They smell delicious."

"I told the military that my factory will be ready soon and we will be making jars of food for them," Appert said, pointing to the steaming pot. "Emperor Napoleon Bonaparte has said that an army marches on its stomach, and my new factory will provide the food for those stomachs."

He turned back to Mae and Clinton and explained, "See, we put food such as stew in glass jars and seal them carefully and then put the jars in boiling water for many hours. After that, the stew will last for months, sitting on a shelf or in an army cart."

"But why do you have to boil them?" Clinton asked. "Isn't the stew already hot when you put it in the jars?"

Appert frowned. "I don't know why it works, but I've experimented with fruits and stews and soups and they all stay fresh and good if prepared by this method. That's how I won the prize—12,000 francs after fourteen years of experiments."

I wonder how much money that is, Mae thought. Aloud, she said to Clinton, "I think heating it in the jars destroys bacteria. My grandmother used to can foods like that."

Appert drew his eyebrows together and took two steps toward her. "Your grandmother! That's ridiculous. Are you here

13

to try and claim some of my prize? And what do you mean by bacteria?"

"Oh, no, you won the prize fairly," Mae said hastily. "Bacteria are, um…just some theory of my grandmother's."

Appert nodded. "The theories of old women, eh?"

Clinton asked, "Could you show us how to seal the jars?"

Appert folded his arms and glared at them. "The two of you must leave at once. I am too busy to have spies trying to steal my process. I wrote everything I know about it in my book."

"Please, sir," Mae said. "We aren't spies. We're students. Do we look like we could start a factory to compete with yours?"

Appert gazed down at her for a moment. Finally he dropped his arms and said, "I am just about to put soup in jars. You two may watch the process, but you must not interfere."

They followed him back to a table near the stove. A kettle of soup bubbled on the stove and a second pot held water full of dark colored jars with wide necks. They looked more like juice bottles than the canning jars Mae's grandmother had used. Appert wielded a pair of tongs to pull three jars out of the hot water and place them on the table. He ladled hot soup into each jar, right up to the brim. Next, he forced a cork into each bottle and wrapped a thin wire around the cork to hold it in place. With a steady hand, he dropped melted wax from a square candle onto the cork to seal the wire in place. Then he repeated the process with the next bottle.

"Once I have eight jars done, I put them back in the hot water pot and boil them for five hours."

"Five hours?" Mae asked. "That's a long time."

14

"It takes a day to produce only a few jars," Appert agreed. "But soon we will have a new factory that will accomplish the job much more efficiently. Hundreds of pots boiling at once! Maybe you will come and work for me."

Mae imagined stirring a pot of stew in a row of hundreds of people doing the same thing, in the steamy heat and delicious smell. Before she could think of a good response, Clinton said, "It would be an honor." Clinton bowed his head slightly. "Thank you for showing us your method, Mr. Appert." He pointed to the pocket where he was carrying the X-PA.

Mae and Clinton left the kitchen as Mr. Appert continued to pour soup into the prepared jars. In the hallway, Clinton stopped and said, "So Appert's glass jars are like our canned food. You know, one time my mom bought some dented cans at the grocery store. One of them bulged out while it was sitting in the pantry and my mom threw it away. She said it might have some kind of disease that I can't remember—but something growing in that can."

"Wait," Mae said. "Are you saying someone on the ship might get a disease from canned food?"

Clinton shrugged. "It's possible. Else why would Selectra send us here?"

"We could ask my mom about it," Mae said.

"Yes. And then we can somehow find our way to the kitchens and check for any bulging cans."

"And save the day," Mae said.

"Right," said Clinton, as he pulled out the X-PA. He peered at it. "Look here, Mae. The button that usually says 'Home' says 'Return to Base.' That must mean the X-PA is tracking the ship. Here we go." He pushed the button.

Nicolas Appert (1749-1841) was a French confectioner and chef. In 1795, the French dictator, Napoleon Bonaparte, became concerned about supplying food to French armies across Europe. Napoleon is quoted as saying that an army marches on its stomach. Most food preservation at the time involved drying, smoking, or pickling. None of these methods worked well for long periods of time. They also did not keep the flavor of the food well.
So the government offered 12,000 francs to anyone who could invent a better way of preserving food.

Appert knew food, so he decided to experiment and win that prize. It took him fourteen years to develop what came to be called the "Appert Method." In 1811, he published a book, *The Art of Preserving All Kinds of Animal and Vegetable Substances for Several Years*. He wrote about sealing soups, stews, fruit or jams in jars and then placing them in boiling water for several hours. If the air was completely removed from the jar and the cork and wax seal held, the food would last without loss of taste.

Appert won the prize money and used the winnings to set up a bottling factory for preserving food. The factory ran successfully for 121 years. Appert never understood that his method of treating the bottles with high heat destroyed microbes that cause food spoilage. But his method quickly became known worldwide.

French armies transported food in Appert's bottles to feed the soldiers. In England, people worked to improve Appert's methods by using metal containers that had to be opened with a hammer and chisel. Today, Appert is known as the "Father of Canning," and food is still placed in metal cans or glass jars using much the same method as Appert's.

Chapter 3
Dinner at the
Captain's Restaurant

Saturday

That evening, Mae and her mom dressed in their best clothes for dinner at the main dining room, the Captain's Restaurant.

"Fancy clothes?" Clinton asked. "Uh-oh. I brought a shirt with a collar. Is that good enough?"

"I think that will be okay, Clinton." Mae's mother replied. "No shorts though."

Clinton rummaged through his suitcase. "Whew. I have a pair of pants. Well, the lower legs can be zipped off to turn them into shorts."

The main dining room had chandeliers and white tablecloths and a man in a tuxedo playing soft music on a grand piano. They found the assigned table that they would be sharing with five other people.

A ship's officer sat at each table, and the captain presided over the table in the center of the room. The officer at their table said his name was Samuel Hammond and that he was in charge of radios on the ship. The couple across the table introduced themselves as Mr. and Mrs. Magione. Mr. Magione had slumped shoulders and a pale face, while Mrs. Magione wore bright makeup and a necklace with a diamond sparkling at the end. "We have our own restaurant. It's having some renovations done this month, so we decided to go on a cruise," Mrs. Magione said in a high-pitched voice. "Our cuisine is finer than you will find here, but what can you expect on a cruise ship?"

The remaining two people worked with Mae's mom in the infirmary and called her "Gina" as if they already knew each other well. They introduced themselves as Dr. Luis Reyes and Nurse Joyce Hilton. Dr. Reyes sat next to Mae's mom and kept offering to refill her wine glass or serve something onto her plate.

Mae nudged Clinton and whispered in his ear, "I think the doctor's hair is too shiny, don't you?"

Joyce Hilton, whose long, light brown hair was pulled back from her face and clipped behind her, sat on the doctor's other side and kept asking Clinton and Mae about school.

When the waiter arrived to take their orders, Mae's mom convinced her to be adventurous and order the quail stuffed with figs. Clinton ordered a hanger steak cooked medium rare.

Clinton's food order came with broccoli, which he pushed to the side.

"What, no vegetables, Clinton?" asked Nurse Hilton.

Clinton made a face. "I really can't stand broccoli. It's so bitter. I don't know how other people like it."

Mr. Magione perked up and looked interested for the first time. "You may be a super taster. Some people have more than the usual number of taste buds on their tongue. They're really turned off by broccoli, cabbage, and Brussel sprouts."

"That must be it," Clinton said, suddenly feeling proud. "I'm a super taster!"

"You can test for it," Mr. Magione said. "You just put some food coloring on your tongue and count the taste buds." He stuck out his tongue and pointed to it, and then he lapsed into silence for the rest of the meal.

At each table a waiter brought over a large bowl of fried rice. Mr. Hammond announced, "This is the winning recipe from this afternoon's adult cooking contest. It's Thai basil fried rice, as introduced to our chef by the winner, Mr. Bouillon." He pronounced the winner's name "Boo-yon."

The waiter scooped rice into small bowls that he placed around the large bowl. Mr. Hammond said, "Please help your-selves to a taste."

Clinton grabbed a bowl, but when Mae jabbed him with her elbow, he offered it to Nurse Hilton before serving himself. Nurse Hilton politely shook her head. Clinton dug in, but he found he only had room for one bite after stuffing himself with steak.

"This rice is very good," Mae's mom said. "A good balance of sweet and spicy."

Mrs. Magione interrupted her. She poked at her bowl of rice with a fork, and wrinkled her nose. "I don't care to try it. The rice is soggy and the smell of the basil overwhelms the other ingredients. The chef who won this round would never get a job at our restaurant."

Mrs. Magione went on about her restaurant and all the fine schools where she had studied cuisine, but after a few minutes, Mae's mom turned to Mr. Hammond and asked how long he had been an officer.

Mr. Hammond smiled. "Five years an officer, but this is only my second cruise on this ship. One of the new features on this ship is high speed Internet," he said. "But when the weather is rough the Internet connection can break sometimes. Actually, the weather on our route may be a bit dodgy, so I need to keep an eye on the network connections."

Clinton perked up when Mr. Hammond mentioned the Internet. "Internet on board? That's awesome. I love being online. Oh, by the way, I made friends with these two kids named Mattias and Riley who were wondering about the ship's networks. Maybe they should talk to you."

"Sure," said Mr. Hammond. "I'd be glad to show them around."

Mae couldn't finish her quail and pushed her plate away. Then she addressed the three medical people sitting on the opposite side of the table. "I was wondering," she said. "What's that disease you can get from canned food? You know, when the cans are bulging."

"What made you think of that?" Mae's mom asked. "Don't tell me you snuck some canned food on board."

"No," Mae said. "I just remembered something about it, and I was curious."

"Botulism," Mae's mom said. "That's the disease."

Dr. Reyes said, "There's a bacterium called *Clostridium botulinum* that can sometimes grow in canned food if there are leaks or it hasn't been sterilized properly. The bacteria make a toxin called botulinus (baw-choo-LINE-us) toxin. It's very rare nowadays."

"What happens if you get it?" Mae asked.

"It can start with diarrhea and vomiting, but the most serious symptom is paralysis. Within a day, the patient starts to get paralyzed, working from the face down. They need to be hospitalized and put on breathing machines, and we give them antitoxin until they recover."

He looked at Mae's mother and smiled. "I say 'we,' but to tell the truth, I've never seen a case."

"A case of what?" Mrs. Magione asked loudly. She seemed to have just noticed that no one except her husband was listening to her.

"Botulism," Dr. Reyes answered.

Mrs. Magione gave a start, clamped her mouth shut, and stared at the doctor as if he had purposely insulted her.

That evening, Mae and Clinton left their cabin to do some more exploring. They wandered through twisting corridors to familiarize themselves with the ship's layout. As Clinton started to turn a corner, he walked right into someone in a white uniform.

"Sorry," Clinton said. "Didn't see you."

"I didn't see you either," the young man said. He had very short hair and was short but muscular, like a wrestler. "What are you doing down here? This prep area is only for staff."

"We are staff, at least sort of," Mae said. "My mom is a nurse for this cruise and we were allowed to come along."

"I'm Heinz," the young man said. "I work in the galley. That's the ship's kitchen."

"Are you a chef, or what?" Clinton said.

"I will be a chef someday," Heinz said. "But for now, I'm a prep cook. I have to follow what the head chef tells me to do. I help to prepare meals. But someday I'll have my own restaurant where I can make what I want."

"Is it hard to work your way up?" Mae asked.

Heinz narrowed his eyes and looked angry for a moment. "I just have to get myself noticed. I had the perfect opportunity if I could have entered the cooking contest on this cruise, but the head chef would not let me. I offered to work extra hours to make up for it, but he said, 'The cooking contest is to entertain the guests with the best chefs, not with some assistant prep cook from East Germany.'"

"Are you from East Germany?" Mae asked.

"That's not the point!" Heinz shouted.

"Yeah, you got shafted," Clinton said. "By the way, is there any food in this area? I'm hungry again."

Heinz gave a laugh that sounded like a bark. "No food around here except in the kitchen, and that's off limits. But you can always go back to your room and order room service. We don't want our guests to starve."

"Aw, come on," Clinton said. "Why not take us to the kitchen? So what if the head chef doesn't like it? He's not exactly your best friend."

Heinz considered for a minute and then nodded his head. "I could get fired, but who cares? Then I'd be free. I can fix you a sandwich. Follow me."

He led them back the way they had come, around two corners and down another set of stairs. From ahead came the clatter of dishes.

"People are working in the kitchen now?" Mae asked. "In the night?"

"Sure, we have to bake and do prep for breakfast now and get things ready for the restaurants tomorrow," Heinz replied. He pushed open the heavy door and led them into a room lined with metal refrigerators, broad sinks and shiny stoves. A couple of other workers lifted their heads and looked over in surprise, but Heinz waved and they returned to their work.

"What will it be?" Heinz asked. "A grilled cheese sandwich with aged cheddar and brie on brioche bread?"

"Sounds great," Clinton answered. As Heinz got out the bread and cheese, Clinton asked, "Do you use much canned food?"

Heinz puffed himself up as if he was offended. "We use fresh ingredients whenever we can. The islands have great markets for fresh fruits and vegetables."

"But still," Clinton persisted. "There must be some things, like applesauce or tuna fish."

"Oh sure, things like that." Heinz pointed to a cupboard. "We keep those over there."

"May we see?" Clinton asked.

Heinz gave him a curious look.

Mae said, "We were studying about canning in school. We're supposed to look for unusual canned items, like...snails."

Heinz laughed. "Go ahead and have a look. I do not think you will find snails."

Clinton brought over a stool and examined the cans on the top shelf while Mae looked at those below. The cans were arranged in neat piles, and he could look them over quickly. Soon he climbed down from the stool, disappointed. "No bulging cans up there," he said to Mae.

She shook her head. "Not down here either."

"What did you find?" Heinz asked, as he laid out their plates in front of them.

"Pimientos," Mae answered. "What are pimientos?"

But instead of listening to the answer, Clinton just bit into the crispy sandwich and the warm and creamy melted cheese.

Chapter 4
Cooking Contest
Round One

Sunday

On Sunday, Mae's mom had to work her morning shift at the infirmary, so Clinton and Mae ate breakfast with their new friends, Mattias and Riley. The ship was going to be at sea the whole day. Tomorrow they would reach their first destination, San Juan, Puerto Rico. The two cooking contests, the adult version and the kids-only version, would help keep everyone entertained at sea.

Clinton tried to convince Mattias and Riley to join the kids' cooking contest with them. "It'll be a lot of fun."

Riley shook her head. "No thanks, I'm not very good in the kitchen. I spill a lot of the ingredients and make a mess."

Mattias said, "Seriously, you do *not* want to be in the kitchen with her. And you especially do not want to have to clean up after her. We'll come cheer you on, though."

After breakfast, Mae and Clinton returned to their room to watch some cooking videos Mae's mother had downloaded onto her laptop. After the first one, an episode where a chef got angry and threw the contents of a frying pan at his assistant, Mae said, "Do you think maybe we should be visiting the next person on the X-PA list?"

"I don't think so," Clinton answered. "That last visit didn't really help us. And we don't know anything about who's getting sick or what kind of sickness they have. Selectra didn't give us any hints except to watch what we eat. What could be a better place to do that than a cooking contest?" He started the second video.

When they were about halfway through the video, Mae's mother came in the door. She was wearing a white coat, but her blouse was wet in front as if she'd been trying to wash something off it. "Hi kids, you here? I hope you had a nice breakfast. Make sure you wash your hands. Now, if you haven't already."

Mae stood with her hands on her hips. "Mom, we're not babies. Did you really come back from the clinic to tell us to wash our hands?"

"I came to change my blouse because someone threw up all over me. Just one day out, and we already have people showing up with symptoms of vomiting and diarrhea. I'm bagging this blouse and taking it straight to the laundry." With that, Mae's mom grabbed a new blouse and disappeared into the bathroom.

When she came out, she looked fresh and neat. Mae said, "Do you think it's norovirus?"

"We can't tell yet. We have to see how people do and whether the cases spread. Meanwhile, just keep washing your hands. I have to go back now." Carrying her soiled blouse in a plastic bag, Mae's mother left the room.

Mae looked at Clinton. "It's starting. Do you think we should go on another visit?"

"Not yet." Clinton said. "Let's do the contest. I have a feeling the sickness is going to be food related."

"As soon as we wash our hands," Mae said.

They headed to the main theater, which had several cooking stations set up on stage. Ten teams of two stood around the stage, wiping hands on their aprons and looking nervous. Most teams were the same age as Mae and Clinton, but a couple of them seemed to be in high school.

The contest host introduced herself. "Hi, you must be Mae and Clinton. I'm Sarah Shires, TV host for the show *Cooking Geniuses*. We'll be taping some of the contest to use on an upcoming episode this season."

"It's great to meet you," Clinton said with a big smile. "I love your show."

"It's always a pleasure to meet a fan." Ms. Shires replied. "We're going to start soon, so you'd better get acquainted with your cooking area."

As Mae and Clinton were reviewing the tools and supplies at the cooking station, Mae said, "You watch *Cooking Geniuses*? You told me you don't watch cooking shows."

Clinton shrugged. "Hey, did you see how happy that made her? It's always better to get the officials on your side." As Mae frowned at him, he added, "Look out there. It's Mattias and Riley, our food groupies."

The theater was mostly full, but looking around, Mae couldn't see her mother. She must still be stuck in the infirmary.

"Ladies and gentlemen, welcome to the cooking contest for juniors! I am Sarah Shires from *Cooking Geniuses*. We have ten pairs of bright, young cooking stars who will be challenged to create a wonderful dish from our mystery ingredient."

Two ship staff brought out a cart with a platter and a silver dome on top. Ms. Shires walked over to the cart and placed her hand on the dome's handle, ready to reveal the mystery ingredient. "We are looking for creative expressions with this popular dried food product, so don't follow the directions on the packaging. Make your own dishes. You have twenty minutes to make something yummy."

Ms. Shires continued, "Our judging panel consists of three cooking superstars. Let me introduce you to our ship's chef from the Captain's Restaurant, Henri Blanc. He is joined by his colleague, pastry chef for the entire ship, Sandrine Childs. And finally, we have a guest judge, Maxwell Bouillion, winner from the first round of our adult cooking contest. He made the recipe for the wonderful Thai basil fried rice you ate last night."

Maxwell Bouillon waved at the audience. Most clapped, but Mae saw a few disgruntled faces. Clinton whispered in her ear, "I bet some of those grumpy ones are people who wanted to judge and get on TV."

Not too far from that group Mae saw some familiar faces, including Heinz the prep cook, Mr. Hammond the radio officer, and Mr. Magione, the unfortunate husband of the bossy restaurant owner. As Mae watched, Mrs. Magione entered through a door near the stage and tottered on high heels past the row of seated audience members to sit by her husband. Mae's attention returned to Ms. Shires when a drum roll came over the speakers.

"And now for today's mystery ingredient!" Ms. Shires pulled the dome from the cart and revealed a pile of small rectangular plastic packages. "Ramen noodles, used by kids, adults, and especially college students everywhere for a quick meal. Your challenge is to make something creative in twenty minutes. Go!"

"I'll get our package!" Clinton leapt from the cooking station and raced to the cart. He returned with the ramen package and ripped it open. Mae started to boil water, but then stopped herself. "We need to be creative. How?" She scanned the other cooking stations and saw quizzical expressions on other faces as well. "What should we make?" Mae asked Clinton.

Clinton laid a fingertip on his chin. "We have to think of it not as ramen but as a package of something else. Let's see, what could we use it for? A sponge floating in the bathtub. A brick for building a noodle house."

"Clinton, stop it!" Mae shouted. "This is serious."

"I am being serious. We have to brainstorm."

"Um. It could be a little boat for floating Legos on."

"Or jellybeans," Clinton said.

"Or we could use it for hamburger buns."

"Now that one," Clinton said, "sounds realistic."

"Once my grandma taught me about baking bread and making pasta," Mae said. "The ingredients were flour, water, and salt. Sometimes eggs. The leavening agent is the tricky part."

"The what agent?" Clinton asked.

"Leavening agents help make dough rise. You can use yeast or baking soda or baking powder to make bubbles in the dough. But we don't have time to let the dough rise. We don't even have dough. We have noodles made of flour and salt and maybe eggs."

"These ramen noodles are curly already and take up a lot of space, so maybe we don't need to make them rise. Let's just put them into a round mold and shape them into a bun." Clinton scanned the ingredients on the table. "If we have a round mold, that is."

In the same moment, they both reached for a can of tuna fish. "Right," Mae said. "Tuna fish can for our round hole, and tuna instead of hamburger for what's inside the bun. That'll save us on cooking time also."

Clinton found the can opener and opened the can. "Healthy, undented can, not bulging," he reported. "At least we won't be poisoning the judges." He dumped the tuna into a bowl and then opened the other side of the can to make a mold.

"Ok, let's split the work. You make a tasty tuna fish patty, and I'll make the ramen buns," Mae said. Clinton nodded and got to work.

"I'm going to add some chilies and hot sauce to the tuna fish to spice it up," Clinton told Mae. "Then I'll add some corn starch and fry them up nice and crisp."

"I'm going to boil the noodles al dente, mix them with some egg, press them into the molds, and then fry them up also. Nice and crispy," Mae replied.

"Be sure to clean the can before you use it," Clinton said. "The outside could be dirty and get into the food." Clinton laughed. "Listen to me. Who would believe I'd turn into a clean freak. But we don't want to be the ones who get people sick on this mission."

Mae tried to juggle in her mind the two things she had to pay attention to—cooking for the contest and keeping an eye out for anything suspicious about sickness. She looked around and saw some of the other team member licking their fingers and then plunging them into the food they were preparing. Yuck! She hoped none of them asked her to sample their creations.

"Focus!" Clinton whispered loudly, and Mae snapped back to cooking contest mode. She pulled the noodles off the stove and packed them with a fork into the tuna fish can mold, which she placed directly in the frying pan. Then she cracked an egg on top. As soon as the combination started to sizzle, she lifted the mold off the noodle bun and made another.

Twenty minutes passed quickly, and soon Clinton and Mae were racing to place their tuna burgers on a plate. "What do we call it?" Mae asked.

"Zwiffy burger," Clinton suggested.

"Or tuna ramen surprise."

"Boring," Clinton said. "It has to be something the judges will remember. I know. How about the Galactic Ramen Melt?"

"I like it," Mae said. She looked up at the audience, and there in the top right, she saw her mother sitting next to Dr. Reyes. She nudged Clinton. "Looks like my mom got a break from the infirmary. Maybe that's a good sign the sickness isn't too severe."

It took another half hour for the judges to try each of the contestants' products. There were ramen pizzas, ramen pastas, ramen salads, and even raw ramen dishes. The scores were tallied, and then Ms. Shires stepped to the microphone.

"Five out of ten teams will continue on to the next stage of the contest, which starts tomorrow afternoon," Ms. Shires said into her microphone. "The five teams that continue on will need to go to the open market when we dock in San Juan to pick up food to cook later in the day.

"The judges were all very happy with the creativity in using the ramen noodles. One day these dishes may even make it to the ship's menu! Please look on the screen to see which five teams are moving forward. Now!"

Clinton and Mae raised their hands in victory when they saw on the screen not only their names, but a photograph of them working furiously with their heads close together. The other team winners joined in with cheers and high fives, while the losers laughed and shrugged it off.

Mae's mom and Dr. Reyes were already gone, but Mattias and Riley came down to the stage to congratulate the winners and to taste the leftovers at the cooking station.

"Yummy," Mattias said as he put some crunchy ramen into his mouth. "I like this much more than just the soup version. You guys were awesome."

"Yeah, that was fun, but now I feel exhausted," Clinton said. "Want to go chill at the game arcade?"

Before Mattias could answer, Mae said, "I really think we should go do some research online to see what we can pick up at the open market in San Juan."

"Are you kidding?" Clinton demanded. Instead of answering, Mae made a motion like a figure eight with her hand.

Clinton got the hint. He nodded and turned to Mattias. "Much as I hate to say it, she's right. We have to prepare for the next round. But let me introduce you to Mr. Hammond first, so he can show you around. Mae, I'll see you back at the room."

On her way back to the room, Mae decided to swing by the infirmary. A line of people sat on chairs or stood in the hallway, some of them clutching their stomachs and groaning. When Mae's mom came to the door to call one of them in, she saw Mae and came straight over.

"What's the matter? Are you feeling ill?"

"No. I just wanted to tell you we made it to the next round of the cooking contest."

"That's wonderful," her mom said. "I'm sorry I couldn't stay for the judging."

Just then, a little girl sitting in her mother's lap vomited loudly, and the awful stuff shot all the way to the other wall. Nurse Hilton rushed out to tend to the little girl, and Mae's mom pulled Mae away from the scene.

"You see how it is down here," Mae's mom said. "Don't touch anything, and go back to the cabin and wash your hands."

"But how did all these people get sick?"

"It shows every sign of a food-borne illness, but we don't know what the germ is or what the food source is."

"It's not botulism, is it?"

Mae's mom smiled. "No sign of paralysis. It's probably just something typical like E. coli or norovirus. Anyway, great job on the cooking contest. Stay away from people who are sick, and have fun."

Dr. Reyes stuck his head out of an office door. "Gina, I need you. This line is getting awfully long."

"Coming," Mae's mom said, and she turned Mae away from the line of sick people. "Go. Now."

Chapter 5

John Snow and the Pump Handle

London, 1854, Sunday

Back at their room, Mae told Clinton about the line of people at the infirmary. "This has to be what Selectra was talking about. We need to get going with our investigation."

"Yeah. I hope the cooking contest wasn't just a waste of time," Clinton said. "Do you think it's norovirus?"

"Let's read up about norovirus when we get back," Mae said. "For now, while we have some time to ourselves, let's go on another visit." She held out her hand, and Clinton passed her the X-PA. "We should start with the guy we skipped yesterday. John Snow, London, 1854."

Mae stepped close to Clinton and waved the X-PA in a sideways figure eight. The spinning sensation took her, and she opened her eyes in a narrow alley. The buildings and people's clothes reminded Mae of scenes from a book by Charles Dickens.

A man in a knee-length coat and what looked like a floppy bow tie walked toward them with a paper in his hand. He muttered and marked the paper as he walked, and Clinton had to jump out of his way.

"Oh, pardon me," the man said. He looked about forty years old, and his brown hair was balding on top. "You see, I am marking my map, and I forget to watch in front of me."

Clinton took a breath. "Are you Mr. John Snow, by any chance?"

"*Doctor* John Snow. After many years of apprenticeship and study I treasure the title. Do you have information for me?"

"Um, no," said Clinton. "Actually, we were hoping to learn from you."

"About the cholera, you mean. This outbreak we're having."

"We're new in town," Mae said, sounding timid and polite. "We don't even know what cholera is. My name is Mae, and this is my friend Clinton."

Snow raised his eyebrows. "If I took you to one of the cholera wards you'd know soon enough. You'd see strong men and elegant ladies tossing on their beds and moaning from the pain as the watery flux pours out of them."

"Flux?" Clinton asked. He wished he'd set the X-PA Translator to London English. Maybe then he could understand what the doctor was saying.

38

"Flux. The contents of the intestine pouring out. Diarrhea, if you will, watery and in large volume, until the patient either slowly recovers or dies a husk of his former self. A horrible death, which is why I have set myself this task of finding the source of the disease."

Mae spoke up again. "That's just what we want to learn, how to find the source of a disease. I'm Mae and this is Clinton, and where we come from there's also an outbreak."

"Of cholera? Where is this place? The Epidemiological Society will send a team to investigate."

"Too much information, Mae," Clinton said. He told Snow, "No, our outbreak isn't cholera. Nothing so serious, we hope. But can you tell us how you're chasing down the cholera?"

Snow looked from one to the other of them, and then he said, "Very well, young students. First of all, do you believe in the miasma theory of disease, that all illness is caused by bad or polluted air?"

"Well, no," Mae said. "Maybe pollution causes some coughs or asthma. But infectious diseases are caused by—"

"Something else," Clinton interrupted.

"I agree," Snow said, "though we do not yet know what that something else may be. Do you hope to enter the medical field, young man? If so, I hope by the time you study medicine there will be new methods to track illnesses to their source, methods that will modernize the field of epidemiology."

"Eppydeemy what?" Clinton asked.

"Ology," Snow said. "The study of how diseases spread, as with this cholera. Look here." He summoned them close and spread the map. "Here, you, Clinton, hold this corner. You see, I have placed a dot on the map showing where each person who became sick lives. Here is where we are standing right now." He pointed. "Do you see a pattern?"

Mae leaned in. "There are sick people all over the map, kind of centered around here." She pointed. "And that center part is where there are the most dots. The most sick people."

"That center area is Broad Street," Snow said.

"So people must be getting sick from something on Broad Street," Clinton said. "From a baker or a butcher or ..." He tried to think of something else.

"There's a pump in Broad Street," Snow said. "Look over here at this part of the map with hardly any dots." He pointed. "There's another water pump right there. A safe pump. A clean one."

"People get their drinking water from a pump on the street?" Mae asked.

"Of course," Snow said, looking at her strangely. "Here in the city, we can't draw our water from a stream, and people don't have their own private wells."

"So everyone is getting sick from a contaminated pump on Broad Street." Clinton added.

"Good job, young fellow." Dr. Snow said with a smile. "Bright lads like you are the future hope of medicine. I've had a horrible time convincing other well-known doctors that there is something dangerous at Broad Street."

"How do you know for sure it's the pump?" Mae asked.

"I ask people," Snow said. "I ask them what they ate, and where they got their beer, and where they collect their water. It's painstaking work. If the patient has died, I ask their families. More and more, the evidence points to the pump."

"May we see it?" Mae asked.

"I'm going there now."

Dr. Snow focused on the map again and started walking.

Mae and Clinton followed a few steps behind Dr. Snow. "We better not get sick from touching anything here," Clinton said. "We can't even wash our hands if the water is the source of the illness."

"Right. Just don't touch anything." Mae said.

After a couple of minutes of fast walking, Dr. Snow stopped and looked up at a street sign. "Here we are, Broad Street," he said triumphantly. He headed toward a water pump in the middle of the street.

Mae and Clinton fell behind as they avoided puddles of water.

"Ack!" Clinton yelled. "Some water splashed on my legs."

"Don't worry." Mae told him. "Just don't let the water get into your mouth. You can only get infected if you drink it."

"How do you know?" Clinton said. "Maybe it's soaking through my skin."

"I'm pretty sure that's not how it works," Mae said. "Let's catch up to Dr. Snow."

The pump stood in the middle of the street. It looked like a thin fire hydrant with a long iron handle for pumping.

Dr. Snow pulled a large wrench from his coat pocket and used it to tug at the bolts holding the handle.

Three large and beefy men rushed to interrupt Dr. Snow. "Stop! What are you doing? We need that water," one of the men cried out.

"It's bad water," Dr. Snow yelled back. "The water is the source of the spreading cholera. It needs to be shut off."

Clinton asked Mae nervously, "Should we help? Those are pretty big guys." Dr. Snow was backing off, holding his wrench.

Mae stepped forward. "Excuse me, gentlemen," she said.

The three beefy men, not used to being called "gentlemen," turned to stare.

"Isn't there another pump you could get water from? One not far from here? And then you can see if Dr. Snow is right, and people stop getting sick."

"You mean someone's poisoned our pump?" one of the men asked. He clenched his fists. "Just let me know who."

"It's not like that," Mae said. "It could just have gotten... dirty somehow."

"Well," said the man. "It looks clean enough. Want to try some?" He pumped a bit of water into his cupped hand and held it out toward Mae's face. "Lovely taste."

"No thanks," Mae said, backing away.

"I would advise you not to," Dr. Snow said.

The man let the water trickle from his hand onto the cobblestone pavement. "Right, tell you what. Me and the lads will tell folk not to get their water here. But if you want to take the pump handle off, that's another matter. You'll need a letter from the Board of Guardians of the parish afore we let you do that."

"And I shall get one," Dr. Snow told him. "As long as my dot maps convince them."

As they walked away from Broad Street, Dr. Snow said, "Thank you for defending me, young lady."

"Women can be doctors too, you know," Mae told him. "I'm more likely to become a doctor than Clinton is."

Dr. Snow grimaced and stroked his chin. "Is that so? I suppose it's possible. But if you do, you'll be the first woman doctor in England."

"Keep an eye out for me, then," Mae said. "But for now, we have to go." She pulled Clinton into an alley and waited while the doctor walked away. Then she pulled out the X-PA and made the familiar loop.

Back in their room on the cruise ship, Mae thought out loud. "Do you think it's cholera people are getting? I wonder if cholera starts with vomiting."

She opened the computer Clinton had been using for some of his games and logged onto the Internet. "Look here," she said. "It says diarrhea and vomiting of clear liquid. Well, what I saw outside the infirmary definitely wasn't clear liquid, but maybe that little girl had to clear out her stomach first."

Clinton said, "You know, Mae, I'm not sure finding the exact same illness is why we're being sent on these trips. I think it's more about methods. We need to make a dot map of the ship."

"What, a map of sick people's rooms?" Mae asked. That doesn't make sense. They're not getting sick from their rooms."

"Hmm," Clinton said. "You're right. It would have to show where they ate or drank."

"Then we'll have to ask them not just where, but what they ate."

Clinton said, "Ouch. That's a lot of work. How are we going to get the deck plans and make the dot map?"

"We'll have to ask Mom for some information," Mae said. "Which means telling her about the project, though without mentioning time travel or G.A.S., of course."

"And maybe Mattias and Riley could help with making the actual map," Clinton said. "They're pretty good with computers, and by now Mr. Hammond will be their buddy." Clinton picked up the receiver of the room phone. "Let me try them at their room." He entered the number, and as Mae washed her hands very thoroughly, he talked to them.

When Mae emerged from the bathroom, Clinton got off the phone. "Mattias and Riley are on board with helping out. They actually seemed kind of excited about it. Mattias said Riley loves a mystery. What if they had adventures like ours?" He laughed. "Mattias said they'll download the maps and meet us later to plot where the sick people have been eating. Now I'm going to take a shower. And then shall we try to get some information from your mom?"

John Snow (1812 - 1858) was an English surgeon, physician, and pioneer in anesthesia and epidemiology. The first of nine children born to a coal worker and his wife in York, England, he was apprenticed to a surgeon at age fourteen. He later went to medical school in London, but did not complete his medical studies until age 31.

Snow learned to calculate doses for ether and chloroform anesthesia, and he administered anesthesia to Queen Victoria for the birth of her last two children. He wrote an early pamphlet on the cause of rickets. An opponent of the miasma theory, which held that disease was caused by bad air, he helped form the Epidemiological Society of London to investigate the causes of cholera. His greatest contribution came when his careful study of a cholera outbreak in Soho led authorities to remove the Broad Street pump handle, which ended the outbreak. It was later discovered that the pump had been set up next to an old, buried cesspit. Snow's studies led to a redesign of water and waste removal systems in London and elsewhere and helped establish the field of epidemiology.

In later years, Snow was a vegetarian and a teetotaler, campaigning against the evils of drunkenness. He died of a stroke at age 45, but his reforms outlived him and undoubtedly saved thousands of lives.

Chapter 6

Growing and Staining Microbes

Sunday

"Why do you keep showing up here?" Mae's mom asked when she looked out in the corridor and saw Mae and Clinton waiting.

"We don't see any patients out here," Mae said. "Is the outbreak over?"

Her mom pushed back a strand of hair and sighed. "Let's say there's a lull. If the lull continues, that will be a very welcome development. For one thing, it will mean we probably don't have norovirus on our hands."

"How would you know that?" Clinton asked.

Mae's mom led them into an examining room and had them sit on the examining table while she sank into a chair. "All I

47

can say is we're pretty sure the source of this illness is some kind of contaminated food."

"Food poisoning," Clinton said.

"We prefer to say food-borne illness. It sounds so much more treatable." Mae's mom smiled. "Once the food source is gone, new people stop getting sick, unless the disease is one that can easily spread from person to person, like norovirus. Norovirus is so infectious that if one person throws up in a restaurant, everyone in the restaurant is at risk."

"What about cholera?" Mae asked.

Her mom looked confused. "What about it?"

"How does that spread? And could this be cholera?"

"Cholera spreads by the fecal-oral route. It's usually found in contaminated water and shellfish. Sometimes there can be an outbreak in a country after a natural disaster like a flood or an earthquake that disrupts the sewers and water supplies." Mae's mother smiled and reached out to ruffle her daughter's hair." I've never heard of it happening on a cruise ship. Besides, these people are uncomfortable, but they're recovering. If they had cholera, they'd just keep getting sicker. They don't have cholera. Not botulism, not cholera."

"So how do you figure out what they actually have?" Clinton asked.

"I'm surprised you're so interested," Mae's mom replied.

"You know us and science, Mom," Mae said. "Research and discovery all the way."

Clinton added, "Solving mysteries every day."

Mae's mom looked back and forth between them. "And poets, too." She stood up. "Well, one way we try to figure it out is by considering the time course of a disease, its incubation period and how long the symptoms last."

"Whoa," Clinton said. "It's ink-you who?"

"Incubation period. How long it takes between the time the bad food is eaten and the time the first symptoms show up. For some toxins it's six hours, and for some parasites it can be a couple of weeks. Now, it's unlikely that all these people here happened to eat the same food last week, before they got on this ship, so we're looking for a germ with a short incubation period— one where they ate something yesterday and started getting sick last night."

Mae nodded. "That makes sense. And we learned in school about John Snow figuring out how cholera came from the Broad Street pump. We thought we'd try to help by working with our friends Mattias and Riley to make a dot map of where all the people who got sick ate their first two meals." When her mom raised her eyebrows, Mae added, "You know, as a sort of extra-credit science project."

"Can we just look at the patient records?" Clinton asked.

"No, Clinton, you may not. Patient records are confidential. But I tell you what. If you stay here, I'll bring a pile of records and read off where the people ate, without names."

"Super," Clinton said. He wondered what was so secret about people being sick. If they were throwing up everywhere, their shipmates were going to know about it already.

Mae's mom returned with a pile of folders and read the information about where the patients had eaten, and in most cases, what their main course was. For some patients, detailed information wasn't recorded. Mae's mom frowned. "I tell you what," she said. "As people get well and leave, I'll ask if they'll let a student interview them for a science project. If we get their consent, it will be okay."

"Great, thanks," Clinton said. He reflected again that this was beginning to sound like a lot of work. He asked, "Aren't there any kinds of lab tests you can do?"

"Yes, there are," Mae's mom answered. "But they can take a while. Shall I show you?"

She led them back through the corridor, where a mother and child were now waiting, and took them to a side door that opened into a small lab.

"Here's an example of what we're looking for," Mae's mom said as she selected a small glass slide from a rack. "It's a standard bacterial preparation to check our samples against. We smeared bacteria on the slide and then stained it. Tell me what you see."

Mae looked at the standard slide through the microscope and fiddled with the knobs. After visits to scientists of the past, she was pretty handy with a microscope. "I see little round things, probably the bacteria, and they're dark purple."

"Here's another standard."

Mae said, "These are pinkish instead of purple and they look like sticks or rods, instead of round spheres."

Clinton took his turn. When he saw the first sample, he blurted out, "These are like what we saw in Pasteur's lab."

"You mean, in the book about Pasteur's lab," Mae corrected him.

"You know about Pasteur?" Mae's mom asked. "Yes, he discovered that foods such as milk spoil when bacteria grow in them. He could kill the bacteria by heating the milk, so that process is called pasteurization."

"But why are some purple?" Clinton asked as he looked at the second sample.

"The purple ones are called gram-positive bacteria," Mae's mom said. "It's a way of identifying what microorganisms are present. All it means is that these particular bacteria take up a certain dye. We add a dye called a gram stain to the sample and the gram-positive bacteria take it up, so they look purple under the microscope. Other bacteria are gram-negative, meaning they don't take up the dye. They look pink. Knowing if the bacteria present are gram-positive or -negative helps to figure out which ones they are."

"Can you show us how to do the staining?" Clinton asked.

"You really want to know?" Mae's mom asked.

"You bet."

"We've been testing samples from the sick people," Mae's mom said. "We've also tested food from the different restaurants to see if anything is contaminated. It can be hard to see just a few bacteria, so we culture the test samples in the incubator. It's a warm oven that allows the microbes to grow on small plates with bacteria food on them. Here's one sample from the first night's fish dish at the Captain's Restaurant that we haven't tested yet."

She put on gloves, pulled a small plastic dish from the incubator, and showed them how to use a cotton-tipped swab to pick up a bit of the sample and smear it onto a microscope slide. "You have to be careful with the dye," she said. "It can really stain your skin and clothes."

"Guess that means we're gram positive," Clinton said with a smirk. "Just like my Gram. She's always positive about everything."

Ignoring him, Mae's mom applied a few drops of dye from a bottle of dark purple solution to the slide, warmed it a bit, washed it with another solution, added another drop of solution

51

STEPS OF

Add a drop or two of the sample you are inspecting to a microscope slide.

1

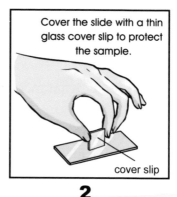

Cover the slide with a thin glass cover slip to protect the sample.

cover slip

2

alcohol

paper towel

6

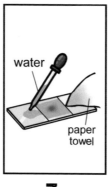

water

paper towel

7

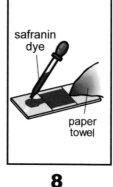

safranin dye

paper towel

8

GRAM STAINING

from a bottle labeled "mordant," and then rinsed the slide with water. After waving the slide in the air to help it dry, she slid it under the microscope and examined it. Then she gestured for Clinton to take a turn.

Clinton squinted through the eyepiece. "I don't see any purple things here," he said.

"No gram-positive bacteria on this one," Mae's mom agreed. "Or gram negatives either. Just a few fish cells. But we'll keep incubating it longer. Something may still grow."

Mae looked and saw several irregular shapes, but no dark purple, just as Clinton said.

"Have you found any answers?" Mae asked.

Mae's mom frowned, walked over to a counter stacked with lots of paperwork, and started flipping through some sheets. "Nothing yet points to a definite cause. That could mean it's norovirus, because viruses are too small to see with a light microscope. Dr. Reyes has inspected the kitchen, but he says it's clean and in top condition. No violations of food safety codes."

"We'll help you figure it out, Mom," Mae said. She held up the sheet where she had copied out where and what the sick people ate. "Let us know if any of these people will let us interview them."

"I will," Mae's mom said. "But what I really hope is that this all just ends by itself, the way most outbreaks do."

"This was way cool, Ms. Harris," Clinton said. "Thanks for showing us. If we want to test more samples, can we come down?"

Mae's mother said, "I don't know if Dr. Reyes would want you using one of these expensive microscopes without supervision. But I tell you what. Last month a researcher sent me a cool new microscope made from folded paper. The guy who invented it wants to create low-cost testing methods for use in developing countries, and he asked me to be one of the thousands of people testing it."

Mae's mother handed Clinton the paper microscope. It wasn't much thicker than a slide itself. She showed him how to use it and said, "Let me know how you find it. The researcher wants feedback on how people use his device for real-world applications."

After dinner, Mae and Clinton went to visit Mattias and Riley in their room. They sat on the bed creating the dot map with the information on the clipboard. About half the sick people had eaten at the Captain's Restaurant, while the other half came from the premium restaurant, the Normandy. Riley called up the restaurant menus on the Internet, but none of the dishes the restaurants carried were the same.

"Maybe it has to do with the same ingredients but in different dishes," Mae said.

"Or a side dish," Riley suggested.

"I bet it's the broccoli," Clinton replied with a smirk. "That way I'll never get sick."

"Tomorrow let's ask Heinz about what goes into these menu items," Mae suggested.

Chapter 7
Clarence Birdseye and Frozen Fish

San Juan, Puerto Rico and Labrador, Canada, 1914, Monday

The third day of the cruise started at the port in San Juan, Puerto Rico. The cooking contestants, both adults and kids, were scheduled to go to the open market and find fresh foods to make the next dish.

"This is my first time in another country, except with the X-PA , of course," Clinton said as he jumped off the cruise ship ramp and onto the dock.

"Uh, sorry to burst your bubble there, Clinton Columbus," Mae said. "Puerto Rico is a territory of the United States. It's not another country."

"Bummer," Clinton said. "Well, it's a beautiful place anyway. Nice and warm."

Mae and Clinton caught up with the other cooking contestants, and Ms. Shires gave them a voucher to buy supplies. The open market had over thirty food stalls with various fruits, vegetables, meats, and seafood. There were all sorts of spices and other food ingredients also. They had thirty minutes to shop, and they had decided to make pizza.

"How about if we spend fifteen minutes separately just looking at food stalls, then get together and decide what to buy," Mae suggested.

"Okay, but if I see something really cool like a shark head, then I'm getting it!" Clinton said.

"Everyone ready?" Ms. Shires spoke loudly. She waited until all eyes were on her. "Ready! Set! Go!"

Mae swerved left and Clinton dashed right. He saw an amazing variety of vegetables and fruits he didn't know. The mixture of scents in the air matched the food stalls' bright and vibrant colors. He averted his eyes from some delicious-looking cooked foods, because the contestants weren't allowed to use anything cooked. And there was no shark head.

"There's an avocado I want that's the size of a melon," Clinton told Mae when they met at the far side of the market.

"Okay, so maybe guacamole topping? I saw a giant pineapple," Mae said.

"We should get some spices also. There are a lot of chilies. I'll get those along with the avocado and meet you back where Ms. Shires is," Clinton said as he started running. "Maybe some other stuff too," he called back.

"I'll pick up a few melons for dessert," Mae yelled after him as she turned back to the stalls.

All the contestants made it back to Ms. Shires on time. "Great job, people!" Ms. Shires said with clapping hands. "Now, let's head over to the cooking area that we've set up outside the ship."

"Why can't we just cook on the ship?" Clinton asked.

"You cannot bring fruits, vegetables, or meats on board because they might be invasive species or carry microbes on them," a deep voice said behind Clinton.

Clinton turned and saw Heinz. "Hey, glad to see you. Is your boss letting you join the contest?"

Heinz glowered. "No, he is not. Chef Blanc is a dull and stingy man. Do you know what he said to me? 'We can't let one of your crazy concoctions destroy our reputation.' What reputation? A reputation for never cooking anything creative!"

Heinz was so angry he was almost spitting. Clinton drew back a little and said, "I'm really sorry he won't give you a chance."

Heinz gave himself a shake, like a dog drying off from the rain. "Never mind, young friend, it's not your fault. I am sent only to help with cooking setup and breakdown."

Mae asked timidly, "What are the invasive species and microbes that you were talking about?"

"Fruits that are part of the natural land here may spread into new locations as the cruise ship travels. If the seeds of the fruits land in the soil of new islands then they may start growing like crazy. An invasion." Heinz replied. "Insects in the fruits and vegetables or germs in the meats could also hop onto another island and destroy its agriculture. On board, we use a mixture of canned, frozen, and fresh goods, but any food that goes aboard the cruise ship has to be checked over very carefully."

"So it's safer just to cook right here and have your ingredients stay here," Ms. Shires added as she overheard the conversation. "Leave your supplies here now. The adult chefs go first, and then you can return for your cooking contest at noon."

With time to spare, Mae and Clinton decided to go back on board the ship and check in at the infirmary.

"Hi Mom!" Mae yelled down the hall.

Mae's mom stuck her head out the door. "Hi, Mae. What's happening with the contest?"

"We have a couple of hours before it's our turn to cook. We wanted to ask you if there were any new sick patients."

"It's calmed down quite a bit. We've only seen two new patients in the past twelve hours," Mae's mom replied. "And I have a whole list of people who are willing to be interviewed by you and your friends. We've also taken more samples from people and incubated them."

"Remind me why you need to 'in cube' them?" Clinton asked.

"Incubate. Remember the microscopes and staining procedure?" Mae's mom replied. "We need enough microbes in the view of the microscope that we can see them, so we have to grow whatever bacteria are in the sample to a larger amount. The number of bacteria doubles every half hour or so, so in the incubator the numbers increase very fast."

Mae's mom walked over to the incubator and opened the door.

"Hmmm. There are a lot of new samples in here. More than I expected. Maybe Dr. Reyes or Nurse Joyce is doing some testing also. I'll check with them later." Mae's mom pulled out her sample. "Let's look at this sample from the premium restaurant."

Mae asked if she could process the sample and carefully went through the steps to stain the slide and put it under the microscope.

"There are a lot of purple shapes," Mae said, lifting her head. "So the gram positive is dominant. And they look more like bats than balls, so I'd say they're rods."

"I agree. We're pretty sure it's either staph or *B. cereus*," Mae's mom said. "Both release toxins that act fast to cause the symptoms we've been seeing. But we still don't know the source."

Clinton scratched his head. "What are the microbes called? Staff and Serious?"

"Staphylococcus, called staph, is a gram-positive coccus, a sphere-shaped bacteria that grows in contaminated meat, dairy products, egg products, all sorts of things, especially if those foods haven't been heated enough or haven't been kept cold enough. For example, sometimes it turns up in mayonnaise at picnics, when sandwiches have been sitting out for a while on hot days."

"But Mae says these are rod-shaped," Clinton objected.

"Yes. *Bacillus cereus* or *B. cereus* is also a gram-positive bacteria, but rod-shaped instead of round. It classically turns up in reheated rice."

"Reheated rice," Clinton repeated. "You mean like the Thai Basil Fried Rice we had the first night?"

"Mom ate it and she didn't get sick," Mae pointed out.

"Be serious, Mae," Clinton said. When she looked confused, he said, "*B. cereus*, get it?" He asked Mae's mom, "Does everyone who eats contaminated food get sick?"

She frowned. "Not necessarily. It depends on how much the people ate, how the bacteria were spread out in the rice, the eaters' own resistance, things like that."

Mae said, "We'll ask around some more when we get back from our cooking contest. Can you come watch?"

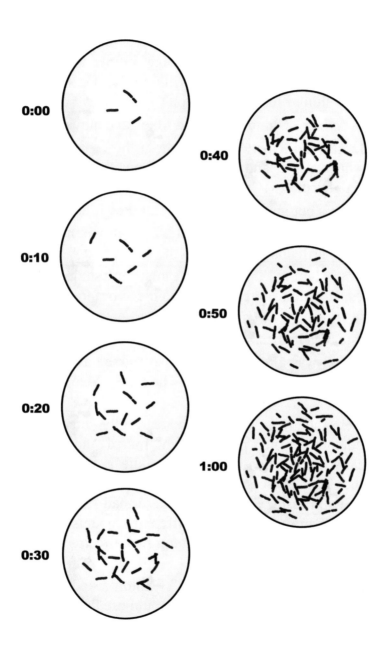

"I'm waiting for Dr. Reyes to get back. We may both come out to see the contest." Mae's mom smiled.

On their way back to the exit, Mae complained to Clinton, "Why can't my mom do anything without that Dr. Reyes these days? I don't think I like him. Do you?"

"*B. cereus*," Clinton said, and Mae gave him a shove.

Mattias and Riley were waiting at the cooking area and began to cheer as Mae and Clinton positioned themselves behind their charcoal grill.

"What's our game plan?" Clinton asked Mae.

"You're the creative one. I'll work on making the pizza dough for the grill and you work on the guacamole," Mae said.

"Got it. I think I'll spice up the guac with some pineapples and chilies." Clinton started to cut into the avocados.

"Be careful," Mae warned. "Don't make something too weird. Taste it as it goes."

Clinton was already spooning soft green avocado into a bowl. "Don't you mean...*B. cereus*?" he asked. Mae stomped on his foot.

Over the next hour, Mae carefully measured out the ingredients for her pizza dough, mixed and kneaded it methodically, and patiently waited for the rising. She added some spices from the open market to the pizza dough edge to give some extra taste. Clinton was like a mad scientist mixing different fruits and vegetables in different amounts in different bowls. After a dozen attempts, Clinton had a recipe for a spicy pineapple guacamole.

"Should we add some meat?" Clinton asked. "I grabbed some pork from the open market. We could use that."

"No, let's keep the pizza fresh and bright." Mae said. "Let's add some cilantro on top. And maybe a squeeze of lemon."

"How about some shrimp?" Clinton said. "I have some of those."

Mae sighed. "You're driving me crazy. Okay, Clinton, we can put a few pieces of shrimp on top."

Clinton spread his guacamole and shrimp over the pizza dough, and Mae grilled the pizza. Of the five teams left, only two would make it to the next round. Mae tried not to think about that or look at what the others were doing. She focused on getting the pizza crust golden brown without burning it.

As Mae reached to reposition the pizza on the grill her hand touched the hot grill grating. "Ouch!" Mae yelled.

"Put some butter on your burn." Clinton said. "My uncle says it will help it heal."

"Not really. That's a myth." Heinz said as he came over with a bowl of cold water and ice. "Just put your hand in here for a few minutes."

"I hope it doesn't leave a mark." Mae said as she put her hand in the cold water.

"We can have your mom look at it when we get back on the ship," Clinton said.

Their pizza was done with five minutes to spare. Mae hesitated to pull off the pizza after being burned, but she took a deep breath and pulled it off using the pizza peel.

Clinton cut the pizza and carried it to the judges' table, where he covered it to keep it warm.

"Sad to say, but we have our first disqualification." Ms. Shires reported over the microphone. "One team's pork dish is still raw in the middle. We are always concerned about food safety, so we cannot allow it to be tasted."

The remaining teams' dishes were a ceviche with scallops and chilies, a fruit salad with a hot and sour sauce, and a roasted vegetable ratatouille.

"The ceviche is fresh and tasty," said Mr. Blanc, the chef from the Captain's Restaurant, making large motions in the air as he spoke. His left hand was missing a finger. "And the pizza is imaginative. Good job."

"I'm afraid the ratatouille is overcooked," said Mr. Bouillion, the first and recent second round winner of the adult cooking contest. "The ceviche I would rate about average, not as good as the one I made this morning."

Sandrine Childs, the Pastry Chef, added her comments. "The fruit salad is colorful and tasty but the sauce rather ruins it in my view. I really like the pineapple guacamole."

Ms. Shires asked the judges a few more opinions before letting them write down their scores.

"We have our two winning teams who will go on to the third and final round of the junior *Cooking Geniuses* contest." Ms. Shires said with a smile. "The two winning dishes are the scallop ceviche and the pineapple guacamole pizza!"

Mae and Clinton high fived each other as Mattias and Riley joined them. "Great job with the pizza!" Mattias said. "Can we try it?"

"Sure, let's see what's left at the judges table." Clinton said as he dragged Riley with him to the table. "Bummer, nothing left."

"We can get something to eat on the ship," Riley said. "Let's head back now. Otherwise I'm going to melt out here in the sun." She put the back of her hand against her forehead and wobbled her knees as if she were about to faint.

After taking some pictures with Ms. Shires and the other teams, Mae, Clinton, Mattias, and Riley headed back to the ship. Mattias and Riley had to go check in with their parents.

"Mae, we've been working all day," Clinton said. "Let's get something to eat."

They chose the Calypso Buffet restaurant for its wide choice of items. As they started eating, Mr. Bouillon sat down at a table behind Mae. He watched them take a few bites and then spoke up. "You probably shouldn't be eating that beef stew, young man."

"Why not?" Clinton asked, turning in surprise.

"The beef for that stew was not frozen before arriving on the ship, and of course you know about all the illnesses. Meat that's been sitting out just may not be safe. For me, much as it pains me, I eat only frozen food from the ship now that the stomach flu is here."

He stuck out his hand to Clinton and said, "I am Maxwell Bouillon, restaurateur of the best establishment in Charleston, South Carolina. I know food and I know what is safe. I also voted for your pizza, young man. And you too, of course, young lady."

Clinton thanked Mr. Bouillon for his vote. Mr. Bouillon went on. "Some frozen foods were brought on the ship before we sailed, so they're safe as long as they stay frozen right up until the moment they're cooked. But I've made a resolution. I'm eating only frozen food or food that I make myself until we get home.

For example, for my ceviche dish in the contest, I handpicked every ingredient."

Mae noticed that he was eating several different vegetables and drinking orange juice. It seemed like a strange meal to her.

Clinton raised his eyebrow at Mae and said, "Are you finished? Time to go."

Mae got the message and gulped down a last bite. She politely said, "Nice to meet you," as they left the table.

"I think I saw something about frozen food on the X-PA," Clinton said. "Kind of like that Mr. Bouillon was talking about. Let's go check it out."

Mae stood next to Clinton while he dialed the X-PA to Clarence Birdseye, Labrador, Canada, 1914. As he looped the device around them, Mae felt sure she knew that man's name from somewhere.

When they stopped spinning, cold air hit Mae's bare arms and legs. She and Clinton stood on a pile of snow near a couple of rough huts.

"Wow," Clinton said. "Didn't think about needing winter clothes on a cruise. This is so different from Puerto Rico." He looked down at his shivering knees.

A man in a heavy coat opened a door in the nearest hut and said, "What are you two doing out there dressed like that? You'll freeze. Come in immediately."

They entered the hut, where a glowing stove gave off waves of heat. The man stared at them suspiciously, waiting. Clinton gave Mae a quizzical look. "We got lost from a cruise ship," he finally said. "An hour ago we were in Puerto Rico and it was hot."

The man looked alarmed. "I've heard of people freezing to death who suddenly go crazy and start tearing off their clothes," he said. "But I haven't heard of them babbling about cruise ships in the tropics." He scrounged around in a big cabinet and pulled out two parkas, a couple of pairs of pants, and some boots. "Here, put these on," he said. "I'm only interested in freezing fish, not people. I imagine your parents will come looking for you soon."

"Not likely," Clinton said. He was feeling cheerful and a little reckless after their success in the cooking contest. After all, why be serious? The thought made him want to laugh out loud. He said, "You're Clarence Birdseye, aren't you? You're the one we came to see. We're trying to learn about food safety and how food is stored and stuff like that."

The man took two steps backward. "Yes, I'm Clarence Birdseye," he said. "Who told you where to find me? I came from the United States to observe the Inuits, these native hunters and fishermen, on a fur-trading expedition. I've learned amazing things about frozen fish."

"Can you tell us about it?" Mae said.

"Are you warm again? Come and see," Birdseye said. In his excitement over his discovery, he seemed to have stopped wondering where his visitors came from.

They walked out into the bitter cold and down to the shore of what looked like a frozen lake. Birdseye led them to a little hut sitting on the ice a few hundred feet from shore and ushered them through the door. A bench ran along one wall inside the hut, and rods and nets hung overhead. Like the cabin they had entered before, this hut had a small stove, but the floor of the hut was ice.

Birdseye picked up a tool that looked like large hand drill and began to drill it into the ice. Soon a hole about one foot wide opened up. Leaning over and looking down a couple of feet, Clinton saw water. Birdseye dropped a fishing line into the water and sat on the bench with the pole in his hand.

"Up here, the fishermen leave their catch outside where it quickly freezes. The temperatures are down to thirty or forty degrees Fahrenheit below zero. I found out that the fish tastes amazingly fresh when it thaws. I want to learn how to do that."

Just then the fishing line tightened up and Birdseye jumped up. He pulled on the line until a large fish with goggling eyes popped through the hole in the ice.

"Let's put this one outside so you can see how fast it freezes," Birdseye said. He quickly gutted the fish and threw the innards into a nearby box. Then he opened the door and laid the fish outside. When he returned, he placed the line back into the ice hole. "Do you want to catch the next one?" he asked Clinton.

"You bet," Clinton said.

Within a few minutes, Clinton pulled another fish out of the hole, a fish even bigger than Birdseye's.

"Check this one out!" he shouted, and he did a little dance the way a football player does when he makes a touchdown.

"Careful!" Mae scolded.

All at once one of Clinton's feet slid out from under him. He did a split on the ice, and his sliding foot plunged into the fishing hole. The cold water cut at his leg like sharp knives. Clinton dropped the fishing pole and yelled "It's cold!" The fish fixed a round eye on him and flopped weakly on the ice.

Clinton tried to push himself upright while Mae grabbed his arm and tugged. "You're pulling the wrong way," Clinton said, but even when Mae let go he couldn't yank his leg free.

Birdseye threw his arms around Clinton in a bear hug and heaved him straight up. Clinton's leg scraped against the ice of the hole and then suddenly burst free.

"There's water in my boot," Clinton said. "It's freezing."

Birdseye said, "You know what you remind me of? Have you ever seen a duck that stood in a puddle on the ice a little too long, until the puddle froze and the duck got stuck? That hole was closing around you, pal. You'd have been stuck there till summer!" He slapped his leg in merriment.

"Mr. Birdseye!" Mae said sternly. "It's not funny."

Birdseye swallowed his laugh. "You're right, of course. Let's take a look." He helped Clinton take off his boot and sopping sock. "What we don't want is frostbite. Does your foot feel like it's burning?"

"Just, cold. Very cold." Clinton said gritting his teeth.

"Hop over here and sit by the stove," Birdseye said. "How about you, young lady, would you like to try for a fish?"

Mae said, "I think we better get Clinton inside where we can dry his foot."

"Inside. Yes. Yes, I agree." Birdseye looked at Clinton sideways. "Um, if you carry the fish I'll get the boot, and I'll carry the boy on my back."

Mae picked up Clinton's fish, which was heavy, and went to look outside. She was amazed to see that the first fish was already completely frozen. Cold as it was, she would never have guessed that the fish could freeze that quickly.

"Is frozen foot—I mean food—safe?" Clinton asked as Birdseye trudged, carrying him across the frozen lake. He could feel the cold air biting at his bare foot with icy teeth.

"If the fish is fresh and good when it's frozen, it stays good. Just keep it frozen until you're ready to eat it," Birdseye said.

"Now I know why your name is familiar," Mae started. Then she remembered that she wasn't supposed to mention the future. "I uh...uh...know someone else with that name."

They tramped up the lakeshore to the main hut. Once they were inside, Birdseye set Clinton on a bench by the stove and tossed him a dirty towel. Little bits of ice in Mae's hair melted and sent cool droplets running down her neck. She squatted beside Clinton and dabbed with the towel at his foot, which was white and cold. When it was dry she tried to warm it with her hands.

Birdseye rattled pots onto the cooking burner, and soon the smell of frying fish filled the room. Then he came over and looked at Clinton's foot. "Don't like the look of that," he said. "Touch of frostbite, if you ask me. Best thing for that is a bowl of warm water. It's a shame I don't have any warm water. But hey, some delicious fried fish will make you feel better."

Mae and Clinton looked at each other. Mae nodded. If Mr. Birdseye was right about freezing, the fish should be safe enough to try. She and Clinton each put a small bit on their plates.

Birdseye scooped fish into his mouth and then said, with his mouth full, "I want to figure out a way to quick freeze fish and maybe even other foods like green beans or corn."

"I think it will work," Mae said. She bit into the fish, and even without spices or sauce, it tasted good, as good as any fresh fish she had ever eaten.

"We'd better get going," Clinton said. "Thanks for telling us about the frozen fish. My foot is burning now," he added under his breath.

"But where can you go in this cold?" Birdseye asked. He stood. "No, no. I really cannot let you leave this cabin."

"Don't worry," Clinton said. "We'll leave the parkas here."

Clinton and Mae shed the parkas, boots, and the pants and piled them on the table. Clinton limped and carried his flip-flops, not even trying to put them on.

Looking increasingly alarmed, Birdseye took a station by the door. "You will have to stay here where you can be safe until a responsible adult comes to collect you," he said.

Clinton looked at Mae, uncertain what to do. Mae took a breath and turned to Birdseye. "I know our parents are out there looking for us," she said. "Could you just maybe go out and shout for them?" As Birdseye hesitated, she added helpfully, "Their name is Smith."

Finally Birdseye nodded and walked outside, pulling the door shut behind him. They heard him calling. "Ahoy there, Smith! We have your children. Smith, ahoy! Your children are safe!"

"Now, quick!" Mae said. "No, wait a minute." She grabbed a pencil stub lying on the table and wrote on the edge of a newspaper, "Don't worry about us, Mr. Birdseye. We are safe. Mae and Clinton." She laid the pencil under the words and took her place beside Clinton as he looped the figure eight. In a moment the warm air of the Caribbean caressed them, and they stood once more on the deck of the ship.

"Oh, man, my foot is killing me," Clinton said. "You got burned on the grill and I got burned ice fishing. What I need is a warm bath."

"They only have showers," Mae said.

"I know," Clinton said. "I'm going to find a bucket. The rest of me can take a shower, but my foot's going to take a bath."

 **Clarence Birdseye** (1886-1956) grew up in Brooklyn, New York. Since he didn't have enough money to attend college, he first worked as a taxidermist and then got a job with the U.S. Department of Agriculture. He worked as an assistant naturalist, shooting coyotes in Arizona and New Mexico. He also helped capture small mammals in Montana for Willard Van Orsdel King, who was studying ticks as the source of Rocky Mountain spotted fever.

Birdseye next went to Labrador (now part of Canada) to observe fur traders. The native Inuit taught him how to ice fish, and he learned that at -40 degrees Fahrenheit the fish froze quickly. When thawed, the fish tasted fresh—much fresher than frozen seafood available in the United States.

Birdseye began to investigate why. Usually, food was frozen at a higher temperature, which took longer and allowed ice crystals to form in the cells of the food. When the food thawed, the cells had been damaged by the ice crystals , and the food had a mushy or dry consistency.

Birdseye experimented with methods to quick freeze fish. He formed a company to produce quick-frozen food, but it went bankrupt because of lack of sales. He developed an even faster method and started another company. His company began quick-freezing meats, poultry and vegetables. Eventually he sold the company to what became the General Foods Corporation. They formed the Birds Eye Frozen Food Company and kept Birdseye on staff to keep improving his process. Today, Birds Eye frozen foods are a top seller.

Chapter 8

Sara Josephine Baker and Mary Mallon

New York City, New York, 1907, Monday

While Clinton was in the shower, Mae pocketed the X-PA and made her way down to the kitchen. She slipped through the double steel doors and caught sight of Heinz mixing a pot on the stove. She walked over to him and said, "Can I ask you something?"

Heinz made a face and pulled the pot to the side of the stove. Then he led Mae back out of the kitchen. "You can't visit me down here. Certainly not during the day."

"I'm sorry," Mae said. "I just wanted to ask you if you have freezers down here."

"Of course we have freezers. Big ones, full of meat and fish and even vegetables."

"Does all the food stay frozen up until you use it?" Mae asked. "Or does some get defrosted and maybe lie around a bit so germs could grow?"

"Not you too," Heinz said. "I've had enough of these questions. That doctor has already been down here poking around everywhere. Not to mention the captain. The answers are always the same. We follow good procedures. We keep the food frozen until the moment we cook it. None of us are sick. We wash the fruits and vegetables. We wash our hands. Our kitchen is clean. Why not stop trying to be a detective and just enjoy yourself?"

Mae walked back toward the room with her eyes stinging, feeling as if she'd been scolded. This G.A.S. mission wasn't going well at all. She'd burned herself and Clinton had acted like an idiot and gotten frostbite. Mattias and Riley seemed too caught up in their computers to be any fun. Visits with the X-PA were getting them nowhere. And worst of all—even though she knew it was terrible of her to look at it this way—worst of all, the sickness seemed to be solving itself without them. Any minute Selectra would appear and ask for the X-PA back. "I'm sorry you failed this mission," she would say.

Mae stopped in a corridor and leaned against the wall. She held up the X-PA and scrolled through the Candidates for Interview. Appert and canning. Birdseye and frozen foods. Both completely beside the point. John Snow and the dot maps for cholera. Well, cholera was a red herring, but the dot maps could still be useful. There must be something else useful hidden in the past. She checked some other names.

Alice Evans: pasteurizing milk.

Cecily Hoover: amino acids and nutrition.

Somehow neither of those sounded like the solution to the mystery.

Sara Josephine Baker, M.D. and "Typhoid" Mary Mallon, cook, New York City, 1907.

Mae's heartbeat quickened just a little. Typhoid Mary—she felt sure she had heard that name somewhere. It sounded mysterious and threatening, well worth a visit. And if Clinton wasn't feeling up to it—if his foot needed a rest—then why shouldn't she go by herself just this once? She would report back anything she learned.

Feeling a little guilty at leaving Clinton out of the trip, Mae made her selection and looped the X-PA.

When Mae's vision settled, she saw a row of houses along a cobblestone street lined with scraggly trees. There were no automobiles in the street, and a woman walking by wore a broad hat and a skirt down to her ankles. The house in front of Mae didn't look like a doctor's office, so maybe it was the house where Mary Mallon worked. Mae decided to look for the servant's entrance around back.

Mae knocked on the back door, and a large woman in a white apron opened it. The woman had a mass of dark hair, and she held a large wooden spoon.

"I'm looking for Mary Mallon," Mae said.

"Ye found her," the woman said. "Are you the new kitchen maid? Hiring blackies now, are they? Well, sit down and have some of my best Guinness pie and apple cake."

At first Mae wanted to yell at Mallon for calling her "blackie" and assuming she was a maid, but she held back. Maybe girls her age really were maids in 1907, and the cook seemed friendly. The baked goods smelled inviting and Mae's stomach gave off a pang of hunger, but she resisted that too. "Actually, Mrs. Mallon, I'm not a maid. I'm a student learning about food safety."

Mallon's face grew red, and she raised her spoon. "Whatever they say, it's wrong!" she cried. "Never been sick a day in my life. They talk behind my back about my families getting sick, but it's nothing to do with me. The families love my food, and these health inspectors are trying to take away my livelihood. 'Do you wash your hands?' they ask. And why should I, when I've never been sick a day in my life? If these upper class snooties get sick, maybe they're weak from never doing a lick of work their whole lives."

A soft knock came at the door and Mallon went to open it. In the doorway stood a woman in her mid-thirties, wearing glasses, with her brown hair parted in the middle and gathered in two buns at the sides of her head.

The woman put her foot in the door and said firmly, "Mrs. Mallon, I must ask you again to come in and give us some samples."

"Off with ye, ye demon!" Mallon answered, and she tried to force the door shut. But it burst open, and Mallon staggered backward as three policemen in helmets and blue uniforms piled into the kitchen.

Mallon squawked and ran for her work table, where she picked up a carving knife. She threw herself on the nearest policeman, beating him with the spoon and threatening him with the knife. But the other two policemen got behind her broad back and caught her arms. Mallon screeched as they bundled her outside.

Mae crouched trembling in a corner of the kitchen until a woman's voice addressed her. "I'm Dr. Sara Josephine Baker, child. Tell me, do you work here too?"

"Oh, no." Mae shook her head hastily. She didn't want to be dragged away. "I'm a student, visiting."

Mary Mallon (1869 – 1938), who became known as Typhoid Mary, was the first person known to be a carrier of typhoid without suffering any symptoms herself. Born in Ireland, she came to the United States at age fifteen, and soon went to work as a cook for wealthy families. Repeatedly, typhoid fever broke out in families she worked for. In all, she infected 51 people, of  whom three died. Each time, she left her job shortly after the outbreak. When contacted, she refused to give samples and angrily denied causing the disease.

In 1907 Sara Josephine Baker tracked Mary down and had her taken into custody. She was found to have *Salmonella typhi* in her gall bladder but refused to have it removed. After three years in a clinic, she promised not to work as a cook and was released.

She found work as a laundress, but soon changed her name to Mary Brown and began cooking again. Wherever she cooked, people fell ill, until in 1915 she started an outbreak at a women's hospital in which twenty-five people became infected. The authorities caught up with her again, and she was confined on North Brother Island for the remaining twenty-three years of her life.

"I hope you haven't eaten any of the food in this kitchen. It will all need to be destroyed."

Mae shook her head again. "Actually, I'm studying food safety. Can you tell me what's going on?"

"We're afraid that Mary Mallon is a carrier of typhoid fever," Dr. Baker said. "Dr. George Soper and I have traced a number of outbreaks of typhoid to houses where she worked as a cook. We have found eight families she worked for, and in seven of them, the family fell ill within weeks of her arrival." Dr. Baker sighed. "I've been trying to collect urine and stool samples from Ms. Mallon for some time, but she pulled out that knife and threatened me if I didn't stay away."

"What is typhoid like?" Mae asked.

Dr. Baker looked sad. "High fevers, severe abdominal pains. Those are belly pains, you know. Most people recover eventually, but both my father and my brother died of typhoid. That's what inspired me to go into medicine in the first place."

"Died!" Mae said. "That's terrible."

"Death motivates me," Dr. Baker said. "Do you know that five years ago we had 1500 infants die each week in Hell's Kitchen?"

"Hell's Kitchen?" Mae repeated, confused.

"It's a New York City slum," Dr. Baker answered. "Where are you from, child?"

"Massachusetts," Mae answered. "Fifteen hundred infants! That's so awful. What can you do about the dying children?"

"We train the mothers about cleanliness, and we give them safe milk and eye drops to prevent blindness in their babies. Poverty and dirt, my dear, that's what causes disease. Dirt and poverty and ignorance. You seem like a bright girl. You should think about a career in medicine. What could be more noble?"

Dr. Baker began peeking into the pots on the stove and spooning samples of food into small vials. Mae looked out the window, where policemen were still trying to get Mallon loaded into a police wagon drawn by horses. She was still yelling.

Mae asked, "What will happen to Mrs. Mallon?"

"We'll test her to see if she is carrying the typhoid germ. If she is, she can't cook anymore." Dr. Baker shook her head. "I don't know if I've ever met a more stubborn woman. If she refuses to stay away from cooking, we'll have to confine her."

"You mean put her in jail?" Mae asked.

"House her someplace where she can be cared for without harming others."

"Isn't there some medicine you can give her?" Mae asked.

Dr. Baker shook her head. "Maybe someday." She loaded the vials of food into what looked like a very large black purse and said, "I must ride along to the police station."

"I have to get back too," Mae said. "Thank you for talking to me."

"Be sure to use that good mind of yours," Dr. Baker said as she left.

When she was gone, Mae walked over to the door and picked up the kitchen knife Mary Mallon had dropped there after threatening the policemen. It was heavy and sharp, and Mae imagined Mary Mallon advancing on her with the knife held high. Who could have imagined that food safety was so dangerous?

Mae set the knife on the kitchen table and picked up the X-PA.

"I can't believe you went without me," Clinton said when Mae finished her story. He was sitting along the length of the couch with his foot raised.

"I know, I'm sorry, I shouldn't have left you out, but I thought with your foot you might need a rest."

"But what if Typhoid Mary had gone after you with that knife? Who would protect you?"

The thought of Clinton protecting her from a large, knife-wielding woman was so astonishing that Mae didn't know what to say. Luckily, she didn't have to wait long for Clinton to add, "Isn't it dinnertime yet? I'm starving. Do you think we should wait for your mom?"

In response, Mae called the infirmary.

"You kids go ahead," Mae's mom answered. "Everything's quiet up here. I'm just finishing some paperwork with Dr. Reyes."

"Do you think it could be typhoid?" Mae asked.

"It's not typhoid. Wrong symptoms, wrong time course. Mae, I think you can stop worrying about this outbreak now. Our last patient just checked out."

"Oh," Mae said, feeling deflated. Then she asked, "Did you ever find out where those extra samples came from? Was Dr. Reyes checking something?"

"He says he doesn't know anything about them," her mom answered. "But now those are gone too. Another mystery has disappeared."

Mae said goodbye and laid the phone on the table. "Nothing new up there," she told Clinton. "Mom's just working late with Dr. Reyes."

Sara Josephine Baker (1873 – 1945) was a physician and public health campaigner. Born to a wealthy Quaker family, she decided on a career in medicine after her brother and father died of typhoid fever. She attended the New York Infirmary Medical College, one of the first medical schools for women, and then passed an exam to be a health inspector. She worked in the New York City schools and in the slum of Hell's Kitchen.

At the time, 1500 infants a week were dying in Hell's Kitchen. Baker worked to provide safe milk and taught women how to breastfeed, how to keep their children clean, and how to keep them from overheating. She also invented an infant formula and made sure that all newborns were treated with eyedrops to prevent an eye infection from blinding them. She campaigned to establish a licensing system for midwives to reduce infant deaths at the time of birth. In the schools, she set up regular checkups for lice and eye disease.

Altogether, Baker's reforms are credited for saving the lives of 90,000 children during her life. However, she is perhaps best known for twice tracking down "Typhoid Mary" to prevent her from continuing her career as a cook.

Chapter 9

Percy Spencer and Microwaves

Cambridge, Massachusetts, 1942, Monday

They chose the Calypso Buffet, hoping they'd meet Mattias and Riley there. Sure enough, their friends waved at them from a table. Riley was squeezing a lemon over a bowl of what looked like seafood stew. "You should try it!" she said. "It's the prize-winning ceviche."

"You mean the one our rivals made?" Clinton demanded, slipping into a seat beside her. "And they're not serving our shrimp and guacamole pizza?" He was surprised by a hot surge of jealousy. Whoa. It was only supposed to be a fun contest, not a huge rivalry.

Riley laughed. "Don't worry, if they served your pizza, we'd be sure to choose that. This is from Mr. Bouillon, the winner of the adult contest." She pointed to the serving line, where Mr. Bouillon, wearing a chef's hat and apron, stood spooning ceviche into bowls. Next to him stood Heinz, carving roast beef.

Clinton and Mae went to get in line. "Hello, fellow champions," Mr. Bouillon greeted them. "You see how they reward me. They promote me from guest to serving boy." He looked very happy as he lifted his ladle and a bowl to offer them a taste.

"I'm not sure about raw seafood," Mae said.

"Did you make this whole huge batch yourself?" Clinton asked.

Behind them sounded the grating voice of Mrs. Magione, the restaurant owner. "Raw food is better than the microwave-reheated soggy food he serves in his restaurant."

Mae asked Mr. Bouillon, "You microwave food in your restaurant?"

Mr. Bouillon didn't answer. His face had turned red, and he spoke loudly to Mrs. Magione, "We've all heard enough about how wonderful your restaurant is. But I am the one winning the cooking contest you didn't qualify for. I'm sure I speak for the other guests when I say we've had enough of your negative comments."

"Negative comments?" scoffed Mrs. Magione. "I've been to your sorry little restaurant. The service, the food, and the hygiene were all sub-par. I'm sure the readers of *Restaurant Today* are going to be very interested in what I found there."

"Don't you dare slander me," Mr. Bouillon said.

"And I will also write a scorching review of the boring, uncreative food on this ship," Mrs. Magione said, glaring past Mae and Clinton at the ship's head chef, Henri Blanc, who stood beside Heinz. "I will demand that my money be returned for this disastrous, disease-ridden cruise and despicable food."

Chef Henri came around the buffet table to confront Mrs. Magione. He spoke in a soft, hissing voice, with little flecks of spit escaping his lips. "You will not destroy my reputation with your lies," he told Mrs. Magione. "I know your type—you have no talent so you seek to demolish those who do."

Mrs. Magione drew back and spoke loudly, turning to address everyone in the restaurant. "Do you see him threatening me? An innocent customer with a legitimate complaint?"

Two ship security guards entered the restaurant and walked silently to the buffet line. Mrs. Magione gave an exaggerated shrug and stalked away while Chef Henri glared after her and then made his way back to his station. The murmur of commenting voices in the restaurant quieted down, and Clinton moved on past Mr. Bouillon to Heinz. "We need to talk to you," Clinton told Heinz. "How about we meet you after dinner by the pool?"

Heinz caught sight of Mae and said, "I didn't mean to be rude to you before, Mae. But you can see why I worry about my boss. He has a very short fuse these days. But yes, I'm off after dinner, and I'll come to the pool."

"I thought they were going to start hitting each other," Mae said when they sat back down at the table with Mattias and Riley. "They got almost as angry as Mary Mallon."

"As who?" Riley asked.

Clinton said, "We're very sensitive and competitive, us creative chefs."

After dinner, all four kids lounged by the pool chatting and watching the ship leave the island. They would be docking at a new island by morning. Soon, Heinz came to join them without his apron or chef's hat. "What's up?" he asked.

"We need your help figuring out what was served where," Clinton said. He opened the dot map and showed Heinz the pattern. Everyone who had gotten sick reported eating dinner either at the premier restaurant, the Normandy, or the main restaurant, the Captain's Restaurant. "But the menus are entirely different," Clinton said. They don't serve any of the same main dishes."

"Let's see," Heinz said. "Some of the ingredients would be the same. Eggs in the sauces, for example."

"Eggs can carry salmonella," Mae remembered. "But this wasn't salmonella."

"I know," Heinz said. "Just like tonight, we made up a huge batch of the winning contest entry. Thai Basil Fried Rice. We served it at those two restaurants, but not here at the poolside or any of the smaller places. It wasn't on the menu because we just added it at the last minute."

"*B. cereus*," Clinton said. They all turned to glare at him, and for a moment he wished he didn't have the reputation of class clown. "No, I mean it. *Bacillus cereus*. It grows in reheated rice." He turned to Heinz. "How do you make it?"

Heinz said, "You start with rice that was fully cooked, maybe an hour or a day earlier. Then you fry it in a wok with all the other ingredients, like vegetables and eggs and spices."

"And then you serve it right away?" Clinton asked.

"If we can. But not everybody comes at once, so"—he lowered his voice—"we reheat it in the microwave."

"Does the microwave get it hot enough to kill any germs?" Riley asked.

"It's already been cooked two times," Heinz said. "As for the microwave, I think it's hot enough."

Clinton leaned forward. "Is there any fried rice still left over?"

Heinz nodded. He looked a little pale. "I could give you some."

"And we can take it up to the infirmary to test it," Clinton finished. He sat back in his chair with a feeling of elation. The stars overhead looked very fine and bright. "I think we found it," he said to his partners.

"Don't come to the kitchen," Heinz said. "I'll bring it to the infirmary."

On their way back to the room, Clinton asked if he could see the X-PA. "I remember seeing something," he said as he dialed through the names of Candidates to Visit. "Look, here it is. *Percy Spencer, Cambridge, Massachusetts, 1942: invented the microwave.* Let's go visit him."

"I'm tired," Mae said. "And you've already solved the mystery. And everybody got well anyway, so it doesn't matter."

"Ooh, bad attitude," Clinton said. "We love learning science, remember? Besides, pretty soon Selectra will be back to pick up the X-PA, and we won't get another chance." He programmed the X-PA for the MIT Radiation Laboratory in Cambridge, Massachusetts, put one arm around Mae's shoulders, and made the figure eight loop around the two of them. They landed in a hallway looking into a laboratory. The lab benches were covered with pieces of metal, wires, and other electrical equipment.

Clinton stuck his head through the doorway and said, "We're looking for Percy Spencer, please."

"Do you have the security clearance to be here?" a man said from near one of the benches.

"Uh ... uh," Clinton stammered.

"We're here to talk about cooking food in microwaves, not anything secret," Mae said.

"I'm Percy Spencer," the man said. He came out and shook their hands. "Why do you want to know about food and microwaves? We're using microwaves for military purposes, not food. I was building a magnetron when you arrived. Who are you?"

"We're students trying to learn about science," Mae said.

"Can you show us your magnetrons?" Clinton asked. "We won't tell anyone."

"This is highly classified work," Spencer said.

Clinton said, "The truth is, Mr. Spencer, we're from the future. We already know about radar and how it helped the U.S. win World War II."

Mae glared at him. Clinton shrugged. G.A.S. recruits were not allowed to tell people about the future, but on the other hand, people forgot about their visits in a few days. The real question was how Spencer would react to such a crazy claim.

"From the future?" Spencer asked. "You're sure we won the war?"

"Yes, but could you show us how microwaves work?" Clinton asked.

Spencer looked at them very closely for a few moments and then said, "Here at Raytheon we build magnetrons to be used in radar. Magnetrons are like big vacuum tubes that generate short radio waves called microwaves. Radar transmits those microwaves out through an antenna. The microwaves bounce off objects and a radar dish detects the returning microwave. With radar, we can detect planes and ships coming from a distance. The military will take as many magnetrons as we can build. I'm about to start testing one we just built."

Spencer snatched a notebook from a table and began turning knobs on a gray piece of equipment. He muttered something about frequency and bandwidth as he adjusted the knobs.

Suddenly, Spencer grabbed the pocket of his lab coat. A brown stain was spreading from the corner of the pocket.

"How did that happen?" Spencer asked. "My candy bar melted. Never had that happen before."

He pulled the sticky, messy wrapping out of his pocket and his eyes went to the equipment on the lab bench. He seemed to have completely forgotten about Clinton and Mae.

"Did the radar waves do this?" he said. "Could we cook other foods?"

Spencer started scribbling in his notebook and called out to a man across the room, "I think I've discovered something. Come and see."

The other man came over, glanced at Mae and Clinton, and then turned as Spencer showed him the melted chocolate.

"Let's try some other foods," Spencer said. "What else do we have that we can cook?"

"I have some popcorn in my drawer," the man said.

"Yeah, that will work great," Clinton said.

"Who are these kids, Spencer? They shouldn't be here. It's classified."

"I know, but they're all right. Not going to tell anyone."

Clinton looked at Mae and shrugged. Sometimes he thought there was something about the X-PA that made strangers trust them.

The man brought a jar of popcorn kernels back to Spencer. Together they arranged the piece of equipment that Spencer had been testing over a box.

Mae and Clinton backed away to another table while Spencer turned the magnetron on. Clinton held his breath until he heard the unmistakable sound of popping. Spencer turned the magnetron off.

"Wow," Spencer said. "It really does work."

He and the other man looked at each other, and Spencer pulled a handful of popped corn up out of the box. Some of the kernels were white, fluffy popped popcorn and others were burned black.

"It really did pop," Spencer said as he showed Mae and Clinton the popped corn.

"I told you," Clinton said. "Microwave popcorn is one of my favorite snacks."

Spencer gave him an odd look, but Clinton just smiled.

Meanwhile the other man hurried back to the lab bench with an egg and a small pan. "Let's try an egg," he said to Spencer. The two of them arranged the egg inside the pan.

"That's not a good idea," Clinton said. "Never put anything metal in a microwave, and that's not the right way to cook an egg."

The two engineers ignored him as Spencer turned the magnetron on. Almost immediately, there came a spark of light, a loud pop, and then a hiss as the egg exploded. The second man yelled, and Spencer hastily switched the magnetron off. The egg had sprayed the second man's face.

"Oh, no, I'm sorry," Spencer said. "We'd better get you to the infirmary so someone can treat these burns."

"Let's get out of here," Mae said to Clinton as they backed out of the door into the hallway. Spencer hustled past them, guiding the other man, who still had his eyes squeezed shut, by the arm.

Back on board the ship, Mae said, "Well, we learned that microwave cooking is really quick. But remember how long Nicholas Appert boiled his canned food? Maybe the microwave doesn't stay hot long enough to kill all the germs. We should ask my mom about it."

"Good idea," Clinton said. "If she's in the room, we can ask her now. If she's still out with her doctor boyfriend, we can ask her in the morning."

Mae punched him in the arm.

 **Percy Spencer** (1894 – 1970) was an American engineer and inventor. Born in Maine and orphaned early, he left school at age twelve to help support his aunt and family. He worked at a mill, and when a nearby mill installed electricity, he transferred there to learn all he could. At age eighteen, he joined the Navy, where he came an expert in radio technology. By studying while standing watch at night, he eventually taught himself trigonometry, physics, and calculus.

In the 1930s, Spencer worked for the defense contractor Raytheon. One of the world's experts in the design of radar tubes, he helped Raytheon win a contract to further develop and manufacture military radar equipment. His staff grew from fifteen to 5000 employees, and during the war his team increased its production of magnetrons from seventeen to 2600 a day.

As he investigated how a magnetron melted a candy bar in his pocket, Spencer experimented with different foods and setups. In 1945, he filed a patent for a microwave cooking oven. The first commercial oven stood six feet high and cost over two thousand dollars. Countertop microwave ovens began to sell in 1967.

Spencer became a senior vice president and a director of Raytheon. He received many honors, including an honorary doctorate from the University of Massachusetts, even though he had never even attended high school.

Chapter 10

CDC and Second Outbreak

Atlanta, Georgia, 2014, Tuesday

Clinton heard the phone ring in the cabin, and he sat up to answer it. Mae turned over in the bed she shared with her mom. Her mom's side was empty. She vaguely remembered a phone call and her mother gathering up her clothes in the middle of the night.

"Not good," Clinton said as he put the phone down. "That's Mattias. Riley's sick. He wants to meet for breakfast and plan next steps."

"I think Mom's already at work," Mae replied. "Let me call her." She pressed buttons on the phone. "Mom, it's Mae. Did something happen?"

"Eight new vomiting patients," her mom said. "One of our first ones has come back again. We don't know what's going on."

"Did Heinz bring you some rice to test?" Mae asked.

"Yes, and it grew out gram-positive rods. Almost certainly *Bacillus cereus*. But there's been no more rice served since Sunday, and that illness only lasts a day or two. So why is it back?" She sounded tired and discouraged.

"Is our friend Riley there?" Mae asked.

"Yes, she is. She isn't feeling well at all, but she'll be fine. Are you going up to breakfast?"

"Yes," Mae said. "But after breakfast we'll come up and see if there's anyone you want us to interview about what they ate."

"I think that would be helpful. We're pretty straight out here, with cleaning, trying to get people to drink something, and hanging IVs."

"Wait," Mae said. "Are you giving them IV medicines?"

"Some," her mom said. "Most food-borne illnesses go away by themselves. But some people throw up so much or have so much watery diarrhea that they get dehydrated, which makes them weak and dizzy. If they can't keep anything down by mouth, we run fluids right into their veins to rehydrate them."

Mattias already had a plate of bacon and Belgian waffles in front of him when they reached the breakfast room, but he was just poking at the food with his fork, not eating. When Mae and Clinton returned with their own plates, he pushed a copy of the dot map over to them. "We have to start adding to this," he said. "The red dots are where Riley ate yesterday. The only place she went without me is the Taco Bar at lunchtime."

96

Mae said, "I think we should start with a new, blank map. Mom says the first outbreak was over, and we know what caused it. This is a brand new one."

"But it has the same symptoms," Mattias said. "Mostly vomiting."

"A lot of food-borne illnesses seem to have the same symptoms," Mae said. "Maybe you can print out a new map. Clinton and I will go up to the infirmary and see what information we can get, and then we'll call you."

"Okay," Mattias said. He stuffed the map into his pocket and walked away without touching his food.

"Do you think I should have some?" Clinton asked, gazing longingly at the waffles Mattias had left.

"I think you should get fresh waffles of your own," Mae said.

"All the patients say you may look at their charts and talk to their families," Mae's mom said. "Here's the pile of charts. You may use this office and let me know when you're done."

"Can we go see Riley?" Mae asked.

"Better not." Mae's mom hesitated. "There's one funny thing. You remember I told you someone had come back a second time? Well, that person's symptoms are different now. She has a fever and bloody diarrhea. That's not *Bacillus cereus*."

"Is she the only one?" Mae asked.

"The new people are a mix. Some look just like the first batch, but there are two more with fevers and abdominal pain and a little bit of blood."

"Oh, boy," Clinton said. "We better get to work."

Mae sat at the desk, copying into a notebook the patients' symptoms, where they ate the day before admission, and the names and room numbers of their family members.

Clinton wandered around the office and looked at the walls. Three diplomas hung there, and he leaned closer to read them. "I really admire your mom, Mae. She knows a lot and she's brave and she works really hard and even diarrhea doesn't bother her."

"It bothers her," Mae said. "She just gets past it."

"Look here," Clinton said, reading another diploma. "Joyce O'Malley. I thought her last name was Hilton."

"Hilton is probably her married name, dummy. And she probably wasn't married when she went to nursing school. Are you going to help me or not?"

"Nurse Joyce O'Malley," Clinton repeated, and then he sat down and picked up a chart.

Mattias helped as Mae and Clinton spent the morning knocking on doors and asking families about where and what their sick family members had eaten for the last three days. On three copies of the ship map, they marked Saturday's meals with green dots, Sunday's in blue, and Monday's in red. Six red dots showed that six of the new patients had eaten lunch at the Taco Bar Monday, and five marked the buffet where they'd eaten Monday dinner. The blue dots from Sunday's meals were scattered widely. And Mae's mom kept calling them with information from new patients.

Mae pulled at her hair as she looked over the dot map with Clinton and Mattias. "There's too much information here," she said. "I've tried to organize it but it's so confusing."

Mattias peered at his tablet computer, which was called a Greenberry. "We need to know what kinds of food carry what kinds of germs," he said. He tapped on the keys of the computer. "No! Internet's out. I knew this would happen. Listen guys, I gotta go talk to Mr. Hammond."

"That was weird," Clinton said when he was gone. "He acted like it was his job to get the Internet going again."

Mae gave a short laugh. "Maybe Mr. Hammond hired him. We're at a dead end, Clinton."

"We found the cause of the first outbreak. We'll figure out this one too."

"But how? We're stuck."

"Maybe we go back to one of those women you say you skipped. Let's see the X-PA."

Mae handed it over, and Clinton scrolled through the names. Some of the candidates who had been there before were gone, but a new one caught his eye. "Look here. Sonia Patel at the CDC, modern day. You know what the CDC is?"

"Sure," Mae said. "The Centers for Disease Control. They investigate all kinds of infections. I think we could use their help."

Clinton made the familiar loop. When they stopped spinning, they stood inside another laboratory, where a slim young woman with long, jet-black braids was lifting a tray of plastic plates into an incubator. When she finished, she turned around and gave a little jump. She had a red dot above her nose, between her eyebrows.

"How did you get in here?" she asked.

"Dr. Patel?" Mae asked. "We're students, Mae Harris and Clinton Chang, here to ask your advice on a case of food-borne illness."

"Has this case been reported?" Dr. Patel asked.

"Not yet," Mae said. "That is, it's a case we're, um, reading about for school. We don't know how it turns out."

"You're not asking me to do your homework for you, I hope," Dr. Patel said.

"Oh, no! We're allowed to consult sources and experts for ideas," Mae said.

"For general background knowledge," Clinton added smoothly. "How do you figure out the cause of a food-borne illness? Can you give us some examples?"

Dr. Patel pointed to a large chart on the wall with lots of texts and small pictures. Stepping closer, Mae saw that the pictures showed clusters of gram-positive and gram-negative bacteria. Each line of the chart represented a recent disease outbreak.

"One in six Americans gets a food-borne illness each year," Dr. Patel said. "Mostly the sicknesses are sporadic, which means they happen one at a time, but sometimes there are large outbreaks, with lots of people sickened from one source. I keep this chart to remind me how important my job is."

"Wow, look at this, Mae," Clinton said. "In 2011, people in thirty-four states got sick from Salmonella that showed up in ground turkey."

"And just a few months ago, twenty-two football players got sick from something called *Campylobacter* [CAMP-ill-oh-back'-ter] from unpasteurized milk."

"Here's one from frozen food," Clinton said. "In 2013, people got sick with E. coli. That's another gram-negative rod, isn't it?"

"You know about gram stains?" Dr. Patel sounded impressed. "Yes, E. coli and Salmonella are gram-negative rods.

The Centers for Disease Control and Prevention or **CDC**, located just outside Atlanta, Georgia, was established in 1946 as the leading public health agency in the United States. In its early years, the agency worked to eradicate malaria through a program of mosquito control through spraying and draining standing water.

As malaria abated, the agency grew to focus on other infectious diseases, including sexually transmitted diseases and tuberculosis. Today its work includes overseeing vaccination programs, investigating environmental health hazards, tracking chronic diseases, and investigating disease outbreaks all over the world.

The CDC today has a staff of about 15,000 and an annual budget of close to seven billion dollars.

So is *Campylobacter*, but its shape is a little different. Do you want to see?" She selected a slide and put it under a microscope that had several different sets of eyepieces so they could all three look at once. "What do you see?"

"They're pink, not purple," Mae said. "And they're curved."

"That's right. *Campylobacter* has a spiral shape, so under the microscope it looks curved or S-shaped."

Dr. Patel put the slide away. "Would you like to know how we investigate an outbreak here at the CDC?"

Mae and Clinton nodded.

"When we hear about a possible outbreak, one of us travels to the site. We try to identify as many cases as we can, and we chart the course of the outbreak."

"How do you mean?" Mae asked.

"We graph how many people first got sick each day. And then we work backward from there to try and make a hypothesis about what could have caused it. Now, most food-borne illnesses have an incubation period of a couple of weeks. That means it's a couple of weeks before the first symptoms show up."

"That's not the case with ours," Clinton said. "I mean, in the case we're learning about, people started getting sick on the second day of the cruise."

"That's very helpful," Dr. Patel said. "It really cuts down on the organisms you worry about. Also, it's a lot easier for people to remember what they ate a day or two ago than a week or two ago."

Mae frowned. "But what if a bunch of people got sick and then well, and then another set of people started getting sick, and it seemed like the cause might be something new?"

"Hmm," Dr. Patel said. "That does sound complex. I think I'd start with a chart of the timing of the two different sets of symptoms. It might be all one disease or it might be two. I think that will help start you on your way to find the culprits."

"Culprits?" Clinton asked. "You mean like criminals? You think someone's doing this on purpose?"

Dr. Patel laughed. "No, no, by culprit I meant the responsible bacteria or virus."

"Like norovirus?" Mae asked.

"Exactly. Norovirus can come on as quickly as twelve hours. It's a common problem in enclosed spaces like a ship or dormitory. The nasty thing about norovirus, which is sometimes called Norwalk virus, is that it's not only transmitted through food and water, it can also be passed from person to person. And the virus stays around for a while, so you can get it from touching contaminated surfaces."

"How long do some of the others take to show up?" Clinton asked.

Dr. Patel pointed to another chart. "It's all right here. You can write them down if you want, or you can always find the information on the Internet. Now, the next set of clues we look at are the symptoms of the illness. Usually there's vomiting and diarrhea, but is there fever? Bad stomach pains? Blood in the diarrhea? Muscle or joint aches? Headaches? All of those can help us make a hypothesis about what the cause is."

"But how do you prove it?" Mae asked.

"By isolating the organism, growing it both from a patient sample and from the food source. But I have to tell you that in most cases of food-borne illness, the exact source is never found. People get better, and life goes on without a definite answer. So instead we focus on prevention. Food inspections, good cooking and storage practices, testing chefs, and frequent hand washing."

Mae asked in a small voice, "Do people ever die?"

"Most healthy people have a couple of miserable days and then recover. But for some, like the very young or very old, or people who are already sick with something else like cancer or kidney failure, food-borne illness can be much more dangerous."

"You must just want to wash your hands all the time," Clinton said.

Dr. Patel laughed and pointed to a dispenser of hand sanitizer on the wall. "I find myself using that a lot. But I don't want to leave you thinking all bacteria are bad. It turns out that bacteria living naturally in our intestines help keep us healthy. Not only that, we've been using microbes for thousands of years to help us make our food."

"What?" Clinton asked. "What kinds of foods?"

"Well, of course, there's yeast in beer and bread. And there are other microbes in everything from cheese to soy sauce to sauerkraut."

Mae asked, "Could a person deliberately add bacteria to food to make other people sick?"

Dr. Patel frowned. "Are you planning to make people sick?"

"No," Mae said firmly. "I was just wondering."

"It's happened before," Dr. Patel said. "In 1996, people at a clinic in Dallas got sick from eating tainted muffins. The microbe was identified, but no one ever admitted to the crime. There have been other cases where the criminal has been caught red-handed."

She smiled at them. "But that's rare. Most outbreaks are due to accidents in the food supply chain. A sick farm worker harvesting grain may accidentally infect some of the harvest. When all the grains are washed together, the microbes can spread. If animals eat some of the grain, they can spread still further."

"It's like a chain reaction," Clinton said.

"That's why we have to work to keep the whole food supply clean and healthy," Dr. Patel said. "And now I have to go back to work. Have I answered your questions?"

"You've been a big help," Mae said. Both she and Clinton thanked Dr. Patel, and then they made their way out into the hall. Clinton pressed the button that read "Return to Base" and swooped the loop around them.

As they stopped spinning, Mae noticed Clinton scratching his head. "What's up, Clinton?" she asked.

"I'm just wondering why anyone would want to make people sick on a cruise ship," he said. "And why this one?"

"Maybe they hate the cruise company or the captain," Mae said. "But really, I don't think it's anything like that. It's like Dr. Patel said, an accident in the food chain."

"You mean two accidents," Clinton said darkly.

Chapter 11

Time Course and Dot Maps

Tuesday

When they returned to their room, Mae and Clinton gathered up their notes and called Mattias. He didn't answer. The Internet was still down, so maybe he was off trying to help Mr. Hammond somehow. So Mae and Clinton worked on making a graph of when people got sick. They marked an X for each person beside that person's first day of illness. Then they decided to break it down into twelve-hour intervals, and finally to use a different color for people who seemed to have the new illness with fever and bloody diarrhea.

"It's definitely two waves of illness," Mae said. "And if the second one is *B. cereus* again, we know around when they must have been exposed. Look, this first batch of people got sick at dinner Saturday night from Mr. Bouillon's fried rice. So if

106

you work back around the same amount of time from the second wave, you get Monday dinner as the source."

"But we ate the same dinner Riley did," Clinton objected. "Except…whoa, she ate Mr. Bouillon's ceviche."

"Wait," Mae said. She pulled out the dot map. "Look at the red dots from Monday dinnertime. Most of the people who got sick ate either at the Calypso or the Normandy." She shuffled through the pages of notes from their interviews. "Some of these mention the ceviche, but some don't."

Clinton was already on the phone calling Heinz. "Listen, sorry to bother you, but this is important. Which restaurants served ceviche last night? Just those two? Oh, and one more thing. Did Mr. Bouillon help prepare the meal?"

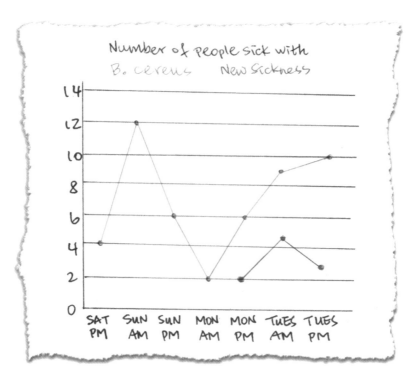

He hung up and turned to Mae. "Ceviche was served in the Normandy and the Calypso Buffet restaurant, just those two. And Mr. Bouillon insisted on helping prepare it, to get the seasonings just right."

"We've got it!" Mae shouted. They both raised their arms in the air and let out a cheer.

"Dr. Patel would be proud of us," Mae said. "We did interviews, made a dot map, looked at the time course, and made a hypothesis supported by all the evidence."

"Yeah, but now we have to confirm it," Clinton said. "I forgot to ask Heinz if there was any of the ceviche left." He picked up the phone again and asked the question. "What, you're saving some for lunch? Bad idea, Heinz. We think it's full of bacteria. Listen, I'll swing by and bring a sample to the lab. See you in a minute."

To Mae he said, "You go on and talk to your mom. I'll catch up."

Mae put her charts in a folder and made her way through the corridors to the infirmary. The hallway outside looked like the first day, with people sitting in chairs looking green, some of them holding seasickness bags. Hastily, Mae entered the lab. There she knocked on the door that connected to the infirmary. Nurse Joyce Hilton stuck her head through the doorway.

"Hello, Nurse O'Malley," Mae said politely.

Joyce Hilton reacted angrily. "What are you talking about?"

Mae hurried to recover. "I'm sorry, I didn't mean anything, it's just I saw your diploma and the name O'Malley was in my head. Um, is my mother free?"

"No, she is not free. None of us are free. Can't you see we have a lot of sick people to take care of?"

"That's just it. We think we've found the source."

Nurse Hilton stared, then pulled the door shut. Mae wasn't sure what to do, but a minute later the door opened and Dr. Reyes stepped in. He said, "Your mother is starting an intravenous line. Some of our patients are getting dehydrated. Why don't you show me what you've found?"

Mae hesitated. The visit to the CDC had raised the possibility that someone was sabotaging food on purpose, and she didn't know whom to trust. Besides, she didn't like the way Dr. Reyes hung around her mother. On the other hand, she was proud of the work she and Clinton had done. In the end, she showed him.

"This is very impressive," Dr. Reyes said. "I was just about to look for bacteria in the patient samples. Would you like to help with the gram stain?"

Just then Clinton entered the lab clutching a brown paper bag. "The last of Mr. Bouillon's ceviche," he said. "Does *B. cereus* ever show up on seafood?"

"We can look," Dr. Reyes said.

Under his supervision, they stained slides with patient samples from the incubator and smears of shrimp, fish, and sauce from the ceviche. Dr. Reyes showed them how to label the slides with a wax crayon and record what they found.

"Definitely gram-positive rods in this one," Mae said, looking at a patient slide.

Clinton examined the ceviche slides. "Nothing," he said. "Bummer. I was sure we had it."

"Let me look," Dr. Reyes said. He bent over the micro-scope and turned the dials, methodically searching every corner of the slide, and then two more. While they waited for him to finish, Mae peered at her slide again with the paper microscope her mom had given her. There was something funny about the bacteria she was seeing.

Finally Dr. Reyes pushed away from the microscope. "You're right, Clinton. I couldn't see anything definite either. But remember, the bacteria may not be very numerous at first. I'll show you how to plate and incubate your sample, and then we can look again later this afternoon or evening."

He sat back. "This is great detective work, kids. There's just one thing. Even if we find *Bacillus cereus* again, that doesn't explain the new symptoms people are having. We've now had another of our former patients come back with fever and severe abdominal pain. There's something more going on."

"I thought so!" Mae said. "Here, will you look at this slide with me? There are lots of gram-positive rods, but I see these funny pink ones too. They're kind of curvy."

"*Campylobacter*!" Clinton burst out.

Dr. Reyes looked at him in surprise. "What do you know about *Campylobacter*?"

"Er, I saw a picture of it," Clinton said truthfully.

"Well, let's take a look." Dr. Reyes slid Mae's slide under the larger microscope and resumed his methodical search. "Yes, you're right. Curved and S-shaped gram negatives. Not very many, but then we haven't been incubating them in the ideal conditions for *Campylobacter*. This is very, very interesting." He lifted his head.

"Can you tell us more about *Campylobacter*?"Mae asked.

"It causes fever, abdominal pain, and bloody diarrhea. There can be vomiting too. And let's see…" He pulled a handbook out of the pocket of his white coat. "Yes. Its incubation period is two to five days."

Mae said, "So the cases you're seeing now didn't come from last night. They came from the fried rice."

"Maybe." Dr. Reyes frowned. "We don't have proof."

"But it's some of the same people who got sick from the fried rice," Mae insisted.

"They got sick with two bugs at once," Clinton Suggested.

"It certainly looks like it," Dr. Reyes says. "What we need to do is re-examine some of those early patient samples and incubate them in conditions that will let *Campylobacter* grow. Then we can look at all our samples this evening. Why don't you come back just after dinner?"

The door to the infirmary opened, and Mae's mom stepped in. "What's happening here?" she asked.

Dr. Reyes answered, "I think these brilliant youngsters have solved our mystery."

"But we haven't solved it, not really," Mae said, as she and Clinton walked back down toward their room. "*B. cereus* in refried rice, that makes sense. But two germs at once? Is Mr. Bouillon some kind of carrier? Or do you think he could be doing it on purpose?"

"I don't know," Clinton said. "But we have a pretty good idea what caused the sickness and what it is. Soon we'll have proof. And then as long as Mr. Bouillon doesn't do any more cooking, people will be safe."

"It's weird," Mae said. "The guy who keeps winning the cooking contest is actually making people sick. What if he's a carrier like Typhoid Mary and has to be locked up for the rest of his life?"

"Or he could just not cook," Clinton pointed out.

"Let's go look on the Internet to see whether someone can be a carrier of *B. cereus* and *Campylobacter*."

"Let's take the day off instead," Clinton suggested.

But Mae insisted. Only when they found the Internet still down did she agree to spend the rest of the day swimming and exploring Charlotte Amalie.

Mae and Clinton met Mattias for supper beside the pool. "How's Riley?" Mae asked.

Mattias shook his head. "She started having these terrible cramps and now she has a fever. She still can't keep anything down. I didn't know the stomach flu could give you a fever."

"There's this bug called *Campylobacter*," Mae began, but she let it trail off. "Hey, any luck fixing the Internet?"

"It's a virus," Mattias said. "I get through for short bits of time but then it goes out again."

"Man, you're really talking like you're some kind of secret crime fighter," Clinton said.

Mattias didn't answer. Instead the three of them went up to the counter to order cheeseburgers. "I want mine well done," Clinton told the man behind the counter, someone he recognized from his trips to the kitchen. "Raw hamburger can have E.coli in it," he told the others. "I saw that on a chart at the CDC." He glanced at Mattias. "Um, I mean, on a chart *from* the CDC, back when we were still getting the Internet."

After dinner, Mae and Clinton invited Mattias to come with them up to the infirmary lab, where Dr. Reyes and Mae's mom met them. Mae's mom told Mae about the four new patients who had come in during the day, while Dr. Reyes and the boys did gram stains and examined slides. Mae heard Clinton give out a hoot of delight. "We got it! We really got it! *Campylobacter* from the ceviche."

"*And* from three different patient samples," Dr. Reyes said. "Now where's the fourth one? Mr. Hu? He's quite sick, but I don't see his plate here. I remember plating his sample myself. Did I take it out and put it somewhere?"

He started looking under piles of papers and behind instruments in the crowded lab, but just then the lights went out. A moment later the backup power came on, but the lights were not as bright.

"Um, can I go say good-night to my sister?" Mattias asked. "Then I have to go work on a…school project."

"I'll take you in to see her," Mae's mom said. "But only you, and please don't touch anything. *Campylobacter* is infectious. It's not like *Bacillus cereus*—it can pass from person to person." She addressed Clinton and Mae. "You two have done a great job. But now, wash your hands, and then go back to the room and wash your hands again. Luis"—she was now addressing Dr. Reyes—"We'll have to let the kitchen and the cooking contest people know that Mr. Bouillon shouldn't be cooking anymore."

As they walked back to the room, Clinton said, "Do you think there's something funny about Mattias? Who does a school project on a cruise? Even you aren't that crazy, Mae."

"No," Mae said. "But we keep *telling* people we're doing a school project, don't we?"

"Just when we're time traveling. Wait a minute. Do you mean to say you think Mattias is from the future, and he's coming back to visit us because we're going to be great scientists someday, and—"

"No," Mae said. "That's ridiculous. I was just thinking, here we are fighting an infection in food, and Mattias is fighting a virus of another kind, a computer virus. I mean, what if he and Riley are G.A.S. recruits too?"

With that question ringing in their heads, they found their way back to the pool for an evening swim.

Chapter 12
Ferran Adrià and Creative Cooking

Barcelona, Spain, 2009, Wednesday

Mae's mother joined them for breakfast in the main restaurant the next morning. To their dismay, Mrs. Magione took the fourth seat at their table not long after they sat down. Her mascara was smeared, and she kept dabbing at her eyes with a handkerchief.

"Where's Mr. Magione?" Mae asked politely.

"He's sick," Mrs. Magione said. "He has a temperature and terrible belly cramps. How could he get sick? We've been so careful! I swear I'm going to sue this cruise company for everything it's worth." She turned to Mae's mother. "Shouldn't you be at work instead of sitting here gorging yourself on tasteless, toxic food?"

"Even medical people have to eat," Mae's mother said mildly. "We work shifts. Nurse Hilton is with your husband now, and I'll be there very soon."

From the buffet line, Ms. Shires, the television host for the *Creative Geniuses* cooking show, waved at them and then came over. "How's our finalist team?" she asked. "I hope you got a good sleep to get your creative juices flowing. I meant to send you an email, but the Internet's still down. We'll need you in the studio at eleven for the last challenge."

"What is it this time?" Mae's mom asked.

"The most creative brunch. We'll have every imaginable ingredient for you to choose from."

"Will the adult contest be going before us?" Clinton asked.

Ms. Shires bit her lower lip. "Hmm. The adult contest has been postponed. We've lost one of our contestants."

"To the sickness?" Mae asked.

"Not exactly," Ms. Shires said, and she turned away.

Mrs. Magione lowered her voice and leaned forward. "I heard they found one of the contestants smuggling contaminated food aboard and using unsanitary practices," she said. "It's shocking. The man supposedly even owns a restaurant. The ship's crew will try to put all the blame on him, of course, but it's their own lax oversight that has allowed the sickness to spread."

"Smuggling food aboard?" Mae asked, but her mom just shook her head.

As Mrs. Magione started to talk again about her excellent restaurant, Mae's mom stood up. "I'd better go see to your husband," she said, and she carried her plate, still two-thirds full, to the counter.

"Um, us too," Mae said. "We have to go practice for the contest." She and Clinton pushed their chairs back.

"Having Mrs. Magione come sit with you would be a great way to keep a person on their diet," Mae said as she scraped most of her breakfast into the trash. "I'd rather starve than spend a whole meal listening to her."

"But look," Clinton said. "For someone so worried about 'toxic' food, she sure seems to be shoveling it in pretty fast."

"How are we going to prepare for the contest?" Mae asked. "We can't watch videos or even look up recipes on the Internet."

"Maybe there's something promising on the X-PA," Clinton said. He pulled it from his pocket. "Look here, a new one. *Ferran Adrià, pioneer of deconstructivist cooking.* What the heck is that? It's in Barcelona, Spain."

"I sure don't know," Mae said. "But I've never been to Spain. Maybe we'll get some ideas."

When they landed, Mae looked over Clinton's shoulder at a building that looked like an old palace. Beyond it, down a hill, shimmered a turquoise sea. "Roses, Catalonia, Spain," read the face of the X-PA. Clinton turned the Translation dial to Catalan, the language of Catalonia.

"That's the restaurant where we're supposed to meet this guy, Ferran Adrià," Clinton said. "I bet he's a great chef."

Mae and Clinton crossed the street and climbed the steps to the front door. They knocked, but no one answered, so they decided to try the back. As they rounded the corner of the building, they saw a man in a white uniform outside the back door.

"Excuse me, sir," Clinton said. "Are you Ferran Adrià?"

"Me, Adrià?" the man asked with a laugh. "I can only dream. The man's a genius. You have business with him?"

"We're students from America," Clinton said.

"Well, I'll introduce you, but he's very busy with some new experiments today."

"Experiments?" Mae asked, but the man had already turned away into the building, so they followed.

Their guide led them into a kitchen full of shiny appliances, many of them unfamiliar to Clinton and Mae. A group of men in white clothes and chef's hats stood clustered around a table. Their guide approached the group and said, "These students are requesting a few minutes of your time, Ferran."

A man with curly hair and large brown eyes emerged from the crowd and turned toward them. "You want to learn about food?"

"We heard that you're doing experiments with food," Mae said.

"Our food here at elBulli is not just food. We mix cooking with chemistry."

"You add chemicals to the food?" Mae asked, wrinkling her nose.

"No, no, not at all. Don't you know that everything we eat, just like the clothes we wear and the air we breathe, is already made of chemicals? I use what is there. I call it deconstructivist cooking. We must be creative and artistic about food and textures, creating new forms that surprise and delight."

Adrià walked over to a counter and said, "Here, I will show you how to make foam. It's my most famous creation."

He pulled out a bowl of what looked like orange fluff. "I wanted to make foams without eggs or cream. Those two ingredients are usually whipped to make foam or a meringue. However, I can achieve the foam effect by whipping a mixture of say, strawberries or mushrooms. If I add the correct thickener, the mixture will have the consistency of whipped cream, but with an intense flavor."

"Mushroom whipped cream?" Clinton said. He had an *Oh, yuck!* look on his face.

Adrià ignored him. "We can also make the foams light and airy by forcing gas into them from this bottle of nitrous oxide. Try a bite."

He handed each of them a spoon and said, "This is one of my recent creations. Tell me what you taste."

Mae carefully took a small scoop while Clinton watched.

"It tastes like carrots," Mae said.

"Very good," Adrià said. "That is exactly what it is. Here's another for you to taste."

This time the object was round and green. "What is it?" Clinton asked before taking one on his spoon.

"It's a spherical green olive," Adrià said. "Try it."

Mae gingerly put one of the spherical green olives in her mouth. She was not sure what to expect, but when she tasted the explosion of olive flavor, she smiled. "I like that one," she said.

"Here is Parmesan marshmallow," Adrià said.

"A marshmallow with Parmesan cheese?" Mae asked. It didn't sound that good to her, but she was surprised at the taste, a mixture of Parmesan and sweetness that was amazing. From the look on Clinton's face, she could tell that he was amazed.

Adrià showed them what different chefs were making. Clinton was fascinated with the man who was using liquid nitrogen to freeze pine nuts. "Why do they have to be so cold?" he asked. "Are you putting them in ice cream?" The man just shook his head and laughed.

Adrià turned to another chef and said, "I think the young man would enjoy Popcorn Cloud. You must eat all in one bite."

Clinton took the tennis ball-sized morsel and managed to stuff it into his mouth. Mae expected to see him chewing, but instead a stunned look came over his face.

"That's awesome!" he said. "It disappears and you taste popcorn."

"Altogether we serve thirty-five courses to each client," Adrià said. "People come to elBulli not merely to eat, but to have an experience with food. That is our gift."

"Do you serve any meat?" Clinton asked.

"Of course," Adrià said. "One of our dishes for today is rabbit with hot apple jelly. Tomorrow we will serve hot and cold trout tempura."

"So how do you become creative? Or how do you tell if a cook is really creative?" Mae asked.

"First, you must truly love food and want to know about all its parts, the smell, the temperature and texture as well as the taste. There are many cooks out there using expensive equipment and techniques that may look fancy at first glance. But, in fact, they are not new and creative. Through experience and analysis, one can examine the dish in question," Adrià said.

"It sounds hard," Clinton said.

"The restaurant industry is very tough and competitive. It takes time and effort and innovation to make a truly creative contribution to the world of cooking." Adrià replied. "Many claim to be creative, but few truly are. Ask yourself, does the dish provide a new experience, new emotions to eating?"

Clinton, thinking about the contest, said, "It must be hard on people if they work really hard at cooking but nobody thinks they're creative."

Ferran Adrià (1962 -) was born in Spain. He first worked as a dishwasher in a restaurant where the chef taught him about cooking. At age nineteen, he was drafted into the army and worked as a military cook. At age twenty-two, he became line cook of elBulli, a restaurant in Barcelona, and a year and a half later, was promoted to head chef for his talent. In 1994, he and two partners expanded the restaurant, and word spread about the creativity of Adrià's work. He is often placed in the category of "molecular gastronomy," but he calls it "deconstructivist" cooking. He takes a dish and transforms it by changing the texture, the temperature or the form, giving unexpected tastes. He is especially known for "culinary foams," created without cream or egg white and often frozen with liquid nitrogen. Another technique is "spherification," in which a liquid with a special ingredient is submerged in a calcium bath to form a flavorful sphere, which can be the size of caviar, an olive, or a tangerine.

elBulli closed in 2011, but Adrià is still top of the culinary world with his books about the restaurant and his recipes. In 2010, he taught a class called "Science and Cooking" at Harvard University. His work has been compared to that of painters and sculptors. Adrià continues to experiment with deconstructivist cooking.

Adrià chuckled. "Chefs are as emotional as other artists. We are full of passion and joy and sometimes jealousy and despair. Don't insult a chef's food if you want a long and happy life."

One of the other chefs came up to ask Adrià a question. Clinton glanced at the X-PA and saw that the Site Energy bar was low again.

"Time to go, Mae," he said quietly. "Thanks for the advice and the warning and the great tastes," he told Adrià.

The chef merely nodded at them, and they went out the back door.

Mae said, "I don't think we learned anything about food safety. But maybe we learned more about creativity. We'll have to take some risks in the contest today."

"Not just creativity," Clinton said thoughtfully. "We learned something about jealousy."

A little before eleven o'clock, Clinton and Mae made their way to lounge on the forward deck where the final contest was going to be held for the junior contestants. They saw Ms. Shires rehearsing her lines and taking photographs with the fancy equipment.

"I'm not quite sure what these things are, Mae." Clinton said. "We should have asked Ferran Adrià to give us a course in equipment."

Mae replied, "I see Heinz setting up. Let's go ask him."

Heinz called to them as they approached. "Mae and Clinton, you wonderful detectives, isn't this a beautiful day?" He beckoned to them to come closer and whispered in their ears. "Germs in fried rice, germs in ceviche, Mr. Bouillon is out, and guess who is taking his place in the contest!"

"You?" Mae asked in surprise. "Your head chef is letting you?"

"Ms. Shires is a very persuasive person. With Bouillon disqualified, she needed a new contestant or the TV show would be ruined. So today I meet my television audience and my true career will be launched!"

"That's so great," Clinton said, but a thought gnawed at the corner of his mind. Who had helped Mr. Bouillon prepare large quantities of his winning dishes? And who had saved the food and sent it to the lab for testing? Heinz.

"Glad to be of help," Mae said. "How about you show us this equipment in return." Mae walked up to the cooking setups.

"Sure, I'm happy to." Heinz replied. "This is a *sous vide* cooker. It's French. It means cooking under a vacuum, but really it's a hot water bath with very precise control of temperature. You put your food in a bag that is vacuum sealed and then put it in the water bath for a long time."

"What can you make with it?" Clinton asked.

"Most cooks use it for cooking meats at a low temperature so that they remain rare but very tender." Heinz said. "There are a lot of science articles about it online. I can show you later, but for a brunch contest like this, I expect most people would use it for cooking eggs to a specific consistency."

Heinz pulled out a picture showing how whole eggs look cooked from 140 F to 160 F in five-degree increments. "You can change how the eggs come out by adjusting the temperature only a few degrees."

Clinton licked his lips. "I love eggs, especially soft boiled. We'll have to do something creative with those."

"What else is there, Heinz?" Mae asked.

"Here is a culinary whipper, also called a siphon," Heinz said. "It's traditionally used to make whipped cream, but people have been using it to make funky foams and to infuse foods with different flavors."

Heinz spent a few minutes showing them how to make passion fruit foam, fruit chunks infused with bubbly juices, and foamy chocolate mousse. "How do they taste?" Heinz asked.

"Amazing!" Clinton said.

"I wonder if we can use chocolate mousse in our brunch," Mae added.

"Let me show you one other culinary technique," Heinz said. "It takes a long time to practice, so I'm not sure if you should use it in the competition."

He put on the table a container filled with a thick but clear liquid. "This bath has calcium in it," he said. "Now look what happens when I drop this liquid into it." Heinz then took a small spoon, scooped out some green liquid, and gently placed it into the thick, clear liquid.

"I bet it's an olive!" Clinton yelled out.

"Hey, how do you know? Have you tried this technique before?" Heinz asked.

"Uh, I must have seen it on a TV cooking show." Clinton said. "But I agree that I probably won't try to do it in the contest. I don't have as steady a hand as you, and we can't afford to mess up."

Ms. Shires came over to their cooking setup. "I see you're getting familiar with the new equipment and techniques. Your competitors over there are getting some help also. We should start in about fifteen minutes."

The fifteen minutes passed. Clinton saw Mattias in the audience, bent over his Greenberry tablet.

Ms. Shires tapped the microphone, and members of the audience stopped talking. "Our finalists are Mae Harris and

Clinton Chang from Massachusetts," she said, as the audience clapped, "and Jacques and Julia Revere from Delaware."

The audience clapped harder. Jacques and Julia were wearing matching *Cooking Genius* aprons. "We should at least have worn the same color tee shirts," Clinton said, clenching his fists. He could hardly believe how much he wanted to win, now that they'd made it this far.

Ms. Shires reviewed the rules for making a creative brunch, and let them know they had one hour to finish. "Ready, set, go!" Ms. Shires said, swinging her arm down as if holding a racing flag.

"Okay, Clinton, so what creative ideas do you have for the brunch?" Mae asked. "Are you planning some weird ingredients?"

Clinton shook his head. "People like bacon, eggs, and pancakes for brunch. So let's do that, but with a twist."

"Got it. So we do soft-boiled eggs in the *sous vide* cooker right at 64 degrees Celsius, but what about the pancakes and bacon?" Mae asked.

"Let's try a cheese pancake made with the culinary whipper and top it with fizzy blueberries infused with some other juice." Clinton said.

Mae smiled. "That sounds *blintzing*, as Selectra would say. And then how about wrapping something with bacon and putting it into the *sous vide* cooker? Maybe shrimp?" Mae suggested.

"Hmm...I don't see shrimp in our ingredients." Clinton said. "Here are some scallops. Try these."

Mae and Clinton split up the work to make their brunch. Mae focused on using the *sous vide* cooker for the eggs and the bacon-wrapped scallops. Clinton worked on the pancakes and blueberries using the culinary whipper. The other team seemed to be trying the technique that used the thick liquid as well as the *sous vide* and whipper. Clinton found himself hoping that Jacques would trip and fall face down in the liquid.

Ms. Shires chatted to the audience as they worked. "And what is your dream brunch? Pickled fish? Papaya cocktail? Sorry, we don't let our junior chefs use alcohol. Which team will make our judges sit up and take notice? By the way, our judges today are our head chef, pastry chef, and Heinz our assistant chef, all members of our prep staff who helped to get everything set up for today. We're happy to have Heinz with us for the first time. He will also compete today in the adult cooking contest."

Mae and Clinton kept checking the clock. The hands seemed to moving much too quickly.

"Five minutes," Ms. Shires announced. "Remember, presentation counts."

"Everything tastes great, Mae. Let's make it all look nice on the plates for the judges."

"How should we arrange it?" Mae asked frantically. "Shall we put the bacon on top of the pancakes or off to the side? If we put the eggs on the plates they're going to run into everything else."

"Just get everything onto the plates." Clinton urged her as he spooned the blueberry mix over the pancakes. "We'll lose if there's no food on the plate."

"Thirty seconds," Ms. Shires warned.

Mae slid the eggs in place and stepped back. "Okay, we did what we could."

Ms. Shires announced, "Time is up. Please stop. Hands up."

The four contestants held their hands up. A sigh rose from all of them.

"Good job, contestants!" Ms. Shires said. "Take a short break while the judges taste your dishes."

Mae waved at her mom, who had joined the audience halfway through the hour. Clinton waved too, trying to ignore the fluttering in his stomach as he waited for the judges to make their decision. There was something else gnawing at him, something that made him uncomfortable.

Mae stood beside him, acting relaxed and carefree, as if it didn't really matter to her who won. "It's great to see Heinz so happy," she said.

That was it. "I know," Clinton said.

Mae looked at him in surprise. "You don't sound happy."

"It's just…well, Mae, I'm feeling really jealous of Jacques and Julia. I feel like I'd do anything to beat them. I was wishing for their meal to be ruined. And I don't even care about cooking. What if I was Heinz, wishing for the chance of a lifetime?"

Mae stared at him. "You mean he had it in for Mr. Bouillon? Heinz planted the germs?"

"He could have," Clinton said. "Look, two accidents don't happen at once. Our time chart suggests some people got *B. cereus* and *Campylobacter* at the same time. I really think we have to consider someone infecting the food on purpose. And who had more to gain than Heinz?"

"But he didn't know he'd get to be in the cooking contest if someone was eliminated," Mae objected.

"How can you be sure of that?" Clinton asked.

Ms. Shires took her place in the center of the lounge and called for everyone's attention. "Please gather together. This has been a wonderful contest, and all our young chefs have put a lot of work into it, but there can be only one winning team."

Mae and Clinton stood next to Julia and Jacques, feeling scruffy in their shorts and tee shirts. Ms. Shires continued, "The judges really enjoyed the creative brunch dishes that were prepared.The cheese pancakes with fizzy blueberries may make it to onto a brunch on this ship in the near future."

Clinton and Mae smiled with hope.

"The judges also found the oyster with the pearl sphere amazing," Ms. Shires said. "It was a tough decision, but the winner of the junior *Cooking Geniuses* contest is…"

Ms. Shires made a dramatic pause. "The team with the best brunch is also the team with the best aprons. Julia and Jacques Revere!"

Clinton's stomach plummeted. He had to fight to keep a smile on his face.

"Let's go congratulate them," Mae said.

"Bummer. Okay," Clinton said. He stepped past Ms. Shires and shook hands first with Jacques, then with Julia, who giggled and bubbled and held onto his hand a little longer than he expected. Clinton glanced over to the judges' table and saw the beautiful oysters, each holding a single white sphere like a pearl that must have been made using the spherification technique with the thick liquid, like the olive.

"They were just more prepared than we were," Mae said in his ear.

"Sure. I know. Let's go." Clinton said.

"Prizes will be awarded at the end of the adult contest," Ms. Shires reminded the audience. "Please return for the final phase of the adult cooking contest at this same time tomorrow."

Mae took hold of Clinton's arm. "Let's get back to work. We have to figure out if Heinz is guilty before that contest tomorrow."

Chapter 13

Identifying the Suspects

Wednesday

Mae and Clinton accepted condolences from Mae's mom. "I'd rather eat cheese pancakes than oysters for brunch any day," she told them. "Sorry I can't stay to have lunch with you, but we're still pretty busy in the infirmary." She shook her head. "And to think I thought this cruise would be relaxing."

"How are the patients doing?" Mae asked.

"The ones who have come back with a second round of illness are really suffering. I think they're exhausted. We're hanging IVs to keep them hydrated. We'll only give them antibiotics if they seem really sick. We're running a little short of IV bags, but we've ordered some more to come aboard this evening."

"Mom," Mae said. "Suppose somebody wanted to contaminate food on this ship. How would you they do it?"

"I suppose they could just try to leave the food out or get it dirty. But for something like this…I suppose they'd have to get hold of a culture of bacteria—two cultures—and sneak them into the food. But honey, nobody would do that."

"Oh, Mom," Mae said. "You just think all people are good."

After they said goodbye to Mae's mom, they looked for Mattias in the crowd. They pulled him aside, and the three of them found a table by the pool.

"Cheeseburgers again?" suggested Mattias. "At least they didn't make us sick."

After they put in their order, Mae and Clinton explained their suspicions to Mattias. "I hate this because he's our friend," Clinton said. "But Heinz has had the opportunity and the motive."

"Does he have a way of getting a culture of germs?" Mattias asked.

No one answered.

"Look," Mattias said. "You have three different things here. One, you think the infections are caused by *B. cereus* and *Campylobacter* in the fried rice and the ceviche. You have good evidence for that. Two, you think that means someone deliberately contaminated the food. What's your thinking on that?"

"Well," Mae explained, "our time course chart tells us the two infections probably started at the same time from the same source. But those two infections don't usually go together. Mom says it's really rare for a person to get two infections at once. The germs don't grow on the same foods or under the same conditions. So the most likely explanation seems to be that someone grew them separately and added them together."

All right," Mattias said. "That's one explanation. And then your third idea is that it must be Heinz because he had motive and opportunity. Weren't there others with opportunity? How about Mr. Bouillon himself? He's the common feature."

"Why would he do it?" Clinton asked. "He's one of the people who has suffered from this. His reputation's taking a big hit."

"Maybe he didn't know he'd be caught," Mae said. "Don't you think it's strange that he hasn't gotten sick from eating his own food? Maybe he knew not to."

"Who does have a motive?" Mattias pressed.

Mae made a chart with two columns labeled "Motive" and "Opportunity" and started to fill it in. "Opportunity," she said. "Anyone who works in the kitchen or the restaurants where people got sick. People who deliver the food to the restaurant. The chefs and the judges."

"They all have the same problem as Heinz," Clinton pointed out. "Where are they going to get a vial of germs?"

Reluctantly, Mae added three names to the column: Nurse Gina Harris, Dr. Luis Reyes, and Nurse Joyce Hilton. Then she crossed off Nurse Gina Harris. "I know it wasn't Mom," she said. Then she moved to the Motive column and wrote down the names of Heinz, the other adult contestants, and Mrs. Magione.

Mattias said, "I don't really know what Mrs. Magione would gain from this."

"Me neither," Mae said. "But she's so mean and jealous I think she'd just be glad to bring other people down."

"She's planning to sue the cruise line," Clinton pointed out. "Maybe she's expecting to get rich."

"Okay, now we have a list of suspects," Mattias said. "Why don't I get the list of kitchen workers from Mr. Hammond.

132

I can also try to do some Internet research on these people's backgrounds if the Internet comes up."

"What can we do?" Clinton asked. "I guess we can ask around in the kitchen and restaurant to see if any of those other people visited the kitchen or handled those two meals."

"Or visited the lab," Mae said. "Supposedly you can only get into it from the infirmary unless someone unlocks that door to the hallway."

"Visited the lab?" Mattias asked. "You think someone's messing with the results?"

"No," Mae said. "But a couple of times my mom or Dr. Reyes have noticed some bacterial sample missing from the incubator. Don't you see? If someone stole the samples, they could use them to contaminate more food."

"Evil," Mattias said. "Okay, Clinton to the kitchen, you to the lab, me to my computer. Meet here at dinner?"

"Oh, sure," Heinz answered when Clinton asked him about any medical personnel visiting the kitchen. "That doctor was down here inspecting before we even left port. And he kept coming again, taking samples here, wiping the counters there, as soon as the sickness came."

"How about Nurse Hilton?" Clinton asked. "Medium height, light brown ponytail?"

Heinz shook his head. "As for the contestants, only Mr. Bouillon came down here." He added, "Sorry you didn't win, Clinton. I voted for you. I thought cheese pancakes were an amazing idea. Want to get up at five in the morning tomorrow and help me prepare them for breakfast?"

"And get blamed if people get sick?" Clinton asked. "No way."

Dr. Reyes let Mae into the infirmary. She saw curtains drawn across the treatment areas where groaning patients lay in bed. The infirmary looked pretty full. "How can I help you, Mae?" the doctor asked.

Mae's mom, emerging from behind one of the curtains with a large syringe in her hand, said, "Mae's got a conspiracy theory."

"Mom!" Mae said. "Remember how you always say 'I treat you with respect and that's the way you should treat me?' This is serious, and we've done pretty well so far."

Her mom dropped the syringe in a special plastic box marked "Medical Waste and Sharps." "You're right," she said. "I apologize. Explain to Dr. Reyes."

"We're worried that someone contaminated the food on purpose," Mae said. "And samples have been disappearing from the incubator. What if the bad guy used your germs to contaminate the food?"

Dr. Reyes nodded, rubbing his chin.

"So what I need to know is who could have gotten in here to steal a plate of bacteria? Do you keep it locked to the outside?"

"Yes," Dr. Reyes said. "No, wait, a couple of days ago I came in first thing and I found the door unlocked."

"What day was that?" Mae asked quickly. She thumbed through her notes. "Was it Monday, the day my mom first noticed some samples missing?"

Dr. Reyes grimaced. "I think so. Could have been Tuesday."

"Anything else?"

"Otherwise the people are pretty much who you'd guess. Joyce, your mom, and me. You and Clinton."

134

"Could any of the sick people have snuck in there?" Mae asked.

"They're too sick. I suppose some member of their family could, but we're always here watching. Sometimes we rush to a bedside for a minute, but they wouldn't have much time. Besides, they'd have to really know what they were doing."

Mae took a breath. "And Heinz, when he brought you the rice?"

"Absolutely not," her mom said. "I met him in the corridor, took the sample, and watched him walk away."

A knock came at the door, and a crew member entered carrying a cardboard box. Dr. Reyes checked the label. "Excellent," he said. "Extra IV fluid. Now we'll be ready for anything."

At dinnertime, the three sleuths got together again. They jumped into the deep end of the pool and treaded water while they talked.

"So the only person we know went both to the lab and the kitchen is Dr. Reyes," Clinton said.

Mae would have been happy to hear this a couple of days ago, but now it just gave her a bad feeling in her stomach. Would a doctor really do something like that? He seemed so helpful and respectful. "Remember Dr. Reyes said the door was left unlocked one morning," she said. "Anyone could have come in then."

"But who unlocked it?" Clinton asked.

"Besides, we have only Dr. Reyes' word that it was ever unlocked," Mattias said. "It could be a red herring."

"A fish?" Clinton asked, confused.

"A red herring is a clue that's thrown in just to get you on the wrong track," Mattias said.

"What about you?" Mae asked. "Did you find out anything interesting?"

"There were just a few minutes when the Internet *was* working," Mattias said. "I found out Mr. Bouillon has a restaurant in South Carolina, just like he said, called *Le Jardin*. It's got pretty good reviews. They used to have a chef called M. Blanc, but he left a year ago."

"Wild," Clinton said. "That's too much of a coincidence. He must be the same guy as the head chef here. I wonder if he was fired."

"That's not all," Mattias said. "I found the Magiones. Their restaurant was closed down for six weeks last year because two cases of botulism were traced to tomato sauce on their pasta."

Mae's mouth fell open.

"Unbelievable," Clinton said.

"Did the people die?" Mae asked.

Mattias shook his head. "They recovered after a few weeks. But even after the restaurant re-opened, no customers came. The Magiones were ruined. They went bankrupt."

"They had enough money left for this cruise," Mae pointed out. "Still, I could see why that would make Mr. Magione depressed and Mrs. Magione bitter. I'd like to see those articles."

"I printed a couple of them out," Mattias said. "But then I thought if I accidentally left them somewhere, which is the kind of thing I always do, we'd give ourselves away. So I tossed them and figured I could just tell you."

"I still want to read them," Mae said. "I might notice something."

"Or maybe you just don't trust me," Mattias said grumpily.

"Don't go weird on us," Clinton said. "Mae's just the type who likes to double-check everything. As in, she never makes dumb mistakes on math quizzes because she always double-checks. Triple-checks, right, Mae?"

"Right, I'll fish them out of the trash," Mattias said. "But now what?"

"The way I see it," Clinton said, "is we have about four main suspects. Dr. Reyes because he has opportunity. Heinz because he has motive and some opportunity. Mr. Bouillon because he had opportunity and maybe now he'll try to prove it wasn't him by starting another outbreak in someone else's food. And Mrs. Magione, because she needs money and wants to sue the ship and she's a crazy angry woman and we don't like her."

"Great reasoning, Clinton," Mattias said.

"Hey, intuition should count for something," Mae said. "There is definitely something wrong with Mrs. Magione."

"Although you'd think she could have protected her own husband," Mattias pointed out. "But whatever. Clinton, you take Mrs. Magione because you're the one who suspects her. I'll take Heinz because I have an open mind."

Mae said in a small voice, "I guess I'll take Dr. Reyes because I can do it without raising suspicions. And I'll try to keep an open mind."

"As for Mr. Bouillon," Mattias said, "I bet a lot of people will be keeping an eye on him, with all the rumors I've heard."

"Done," Clinton said. "Let's have dinner at the Taco Bar and watch the ship depart from the island. Then we can get to work."

As they watched the island slip away they could see the skies growing darker with clouds.

Chapter 14

Tailing the Suspects

Thursday

At breakfast the next morning, Mae, Clinton, and Mattias met to review their assignments. They would be at sea all day, and crew members went from table to table warning guests to expect rough weather. "We're asking guests to stay inside today," a young ensign told them. "A hurricane is passing to the south of us, and we're taking a detour to avoid it."

The final adult cooking contest was still scheduled for that afternoon. "We're going to have to hurry," Mae said. "Our villain seems to go after adult contest winners."

"Or maybe just after Mr. Bouillon," Mattias pointed out. "I'll try to find out if Bouillon has enemies. Meanwhile I'm going up to see Riley. Mae, since you're following Dr. Reyes, do you want to come along?"

When they had left, Clinton checked through the different breakfast rooms, asking the staff if they'd seen Mrs. Magione, the person he was supposed to follow today. The staff rolled their eyes at the sound of her name and said they hadn't seen her yet, so he waited by the window in the Calypso Buffet until he heard her loud, complaining voice. "These scrambled eggs are soggy. And how do I know they aren't poison like everything else?"

Clinton wished he had a newspaper to hide behind like a real spy, but he twiddled his thumbs and gazed out at the glowering sky until Mrs. Magione pushed her chair back and stood. He wandered out of the restaurant after her, waited outside her room, and finally trailed her to the infirmary. "I've come to see my husband," she announced as she walked in.

Mae, who was standing talking to her mother, looked surprised when Clinton joined them. "Dr. Reyes isn't here yet, and Mattias is visiting Riley," she said. "They're talking about computers and something they call a Fix-it Stick. But Mom says Riley had a fever last night."

"We're going to start an IV on her this morning," Mae's mom said. "With the fever, she'll get dehydrated even faster."

Mrs. Magione came out of the curtained-off area where her husband lay sick. Tears streaked her face, and she took Mae's mom by the hand. "My Bernie's not strong," she said. "I told you he has a blood disease. This is too much for him. Please help him."

"We'll do everything we can," Mae's mom said in a soothing voice. "We'll keep him safe."

Mrs. Magione clutched her purse. "Where's Joyce?"

"You mean Nurse Hilton?" Mae's mom asked.

"Yes, Joyce. I want her to look in on him."

Mae's mom said, "Nurse Hilton took the late shift, so she'll be coming in a bit later. I'll be sure to pass on your request, and until Nurse Hilton gets here, I'll check on your husband frequently."

Mrs. Magione dabbed her eyes and walked away. Clinton raised his eyebrows at Mae and followed. Mae tried to figure out what the raised eyebrows meant. Did it mean, *Wow, Mrs. Magione really cares about her husband and she'd never hurt him, so she must be innocent?* Or did it mean, *Wasn't that weird the way she called Nurse Hilton Joyce and asked for her especially?*

"I think I'll go in the laboratory and chart the new patients," Mae told her mom.

Her mom smiled. "Are you sure you don't mean you're going to guard the specimens so nobody steals anything?"

"Maybe," Mae said.

Mae checked that the door from the lab to the corridor was locked. Then she checked all the plates in the incubator and wrote down their labels in her notebook so she would be able to tell later if any went missing. Just as she finished, Dr. Reyes stuck his head in through the doorway. "Working already?" he said. "Want to put on a white coat and come on rounds with me?"

"Sure," said Mae, jumping up. After all, her namesake, Mae Jemison, was a doctor as well as an astronaut.

There were twelve patients filling the infirmary's beds. One of them was a five-year-old boy with an asthma attack. "We think he may have had an allergic reaction to shrimp," Dr. Reyes said. After he listened to the boy's chest with his stethoscope, he told the boy's mother, "His chest is clear. You can take him home now. Nurse Harris will give you instructions."

The rest of the patients were all in for some combination of nausea, vomiting, diarrhea, fever, and abdominal pain. Two were feeling better and ready for discharge, but as for the others, Mae thought she'd never seen nine more miserable people. Riley gave her a weak wave and a grin, but Mr. Magione just lay on his side, groaning. Four of the people were already hooked up to IVs.

When they had finished seeing the patients, Dr. Reyes told Mae's mother, "You're right, beds five and seven both need IVs. Beds two and nine too, to be safe. Magione's looking bad. I'm worried about him and the pregnant lady in bed two. If we were in port I'd think about transferring them to a hospital."

"I'll get started on the IVs," Mae's mom said. "Where's that box that came aboard yesterday?" She dragged the box from the supply closet.

Mae helped her slit the box open with a pair of scissors, and her mom pulled out the first IV bag. Mae's mom let out an exclamation and sat back on her heels. "What's this?" she said. "This is the wrong kind of fluid. Luis!"

Dr. Reyes came over, and they emptied the box. Dr. Reyes cursed twice and then said, "It's my fault. I should have checked these when they first came aboard. Well, for now we'll just have to ration IV fluid. Start Mr. Magione and the pregnant lady in bed two. The others will have to wait."

"What about Riley?" Mae squeaked.

"We'll get her family up here to see if they can get her to drink enough," Dr. Reyes said.

"I'll call them," Mae volunteered.

"Thank you," Dr. Reyes said. Then he addressed Mae's mom. "I'll go ask the captain if we can make our way to the next port a little faster."

Mae withdrew into the lab and called Mattias. "They want someone from your family to sit with Riley and give her fluids."

"Are they worried about her?" Mattias asked.

Mae thought about how to answer. "They just want to help her feel better," she said.

"Okay," Mattias said. "I'll let my mother know. I think I'm making progress here in the kitchen. I'm making friends with the delivery guys who carry up all the food. How about you?"

Mae sighed. "I just can't believe Dr. Reyes would make people sick. He's working so hard to get them better."

"Maybe he just wants a chance to be a hero in your mom's eyes."

Great, Mae thought. Even Mattias notices this thing between Mom and Dr. Reyes.

"The thing is," Mattias said, "that incubator is still the best possible source of bacteria we have."

"Yeah, I know." Mae sighed. "Tell you what, I'll watch Riley till your mom comes."

Mae was still sitting with Riley, urging her to drink sips of ginger ale, when Dr. Reyes returned accompanied by someone else.

"I'm sorry, sir," the doctor's voice said beyond the curtain. "We can't have you out on the bridge throwing up and infecting everybody else."

Mae peeped through the curtain. It was the ship captain, red-faced and bearded. "Let me just take your temperature, sir," Mae's mom said.

After Riley's mother arrived, Mae returned to her post in the lab, sitting quietly at a desk in the corner. She pulled down one of the medical texts and tried to read it, but ended up mostly looking at gross photographs of skin disease. Around eleven, a noise across the room made her raise her head. It was Joyce

Hilton with her hand on the incubator door. Mae turned in her chair, and it squeaked.

Nurse Hilton jumped. "What are you doing there?" she demanded.

"Studying," Mae said. "Are you checking the cultures?"

"No, no, I was looking for my lunch in the refrigerator," Nurse Hilton said, moving her hand to the door of the refrigerator that stood next to the incubator.

"You keep your lunch in *there*?" Mae asked. "With all the urine specimens and stuff?"

"Yes—no—it doesn't seem to be here," Nurse Hilton answered. "I must have left it in my room." She left the lab, looking back over her shoulder at Mae.

Very strange, Mae thought. She entered the infirmary and waited until her mother appeared from behind one of the curtains.

"Does Nurse Hilton keep her lunch in the lab refrigerator?" Mae asked her mom.

"I don't think so. Why should she? As part of our work package we can always call up fresh room service, free. Besides, Nurse Hilton isn't even on duty today until four."

"She's the one, Mom," Mae said. "She was about to take something from the incubator until she saw me. She snuck in and out of here without you or Dr. Reyes even seeing her."

Mae's mom looked troubled. She pressed a hand to her stomach. "This is a very serious accusation, Mae. Did you actually see her remove something from the incubator?"

"No, Mom, I told you. She saw me too soon."

"Honey, we can't do anything without proof. I'll talk to Luis, I mean Dr. Reyes. I tell you what. We'll lock the lab door to the infirmary as well as to the hallway."

"Who has keys?"

"Just Dr. Reyes and me and…Joyce Hilton."

"You'll have to take her keys away, Mom."

Mae's mom wiped her wrist across her forehead and said sadly, "Yes, yes." She changed the subject. "Have you washed your hands, Mae? I'd like you to go back to the cabin and take a shower." She spoke more rapidly. "You've been spending too much time here. Why don't you go down and spend some time with your friends? You'll have to stay indoors. The weather is getting worse. Did you know there's a hurricane passing to the south? We can't get ashore for more IV fluid. Dr. Reyes and the captain have ordered a helicopter delivery."

The three sleuths met for lunch in the buffet restaurant. Through the window they could see flying spray against gray sky. Across the room sat Mrs. Magione, gesturing and talking. From time to time her voice broke through, but they couldn't hear what she said.

Mae, Clinton, and Mattias compared notes. "I know it's Joyce Hilton raiding the incubator," Mae said. "I practically caught her red-handed."

"Mrs. Magione visited her husband and then went back to her room," Clinton said. "She didn't come out again until just now for lunch. I don't think she's having much fun on this cruise."

Mattias sat forward. "Well, Heinz just cooked all morning. He was whistling and practically dancing and couldn't stop talking about his great luck. But then he threw me out of the kitchen, so I just made friends with all the stewards coming in and out. You know, the guys that deliver room service. They also help deliver the meals to the restaurants. One of them told me that a certain passenger is really chatty and friendly and considerate and has even helped them arrange the food a couple of times. Guess who it is?"

"Chatty, yes. Friendly and considerate, no. It can't be her," Clinton said, looking across at the table where Mrs. Magione's tablemates were excusing themselves.

"It is! Mrs. Magione. They couldn't remember the exact dates, but they remember the two restaurants, the Normandy and here at the Calypso."

"Oh, man," Clinton said. "Now we have two ends of opportunity, Nurse Hilton to pick up the bacteria and Mrs. Magione to contaminate the food. But we don't have a connection between them."

"She called her Joyce," Mae said. "Remember this morning, Mrs. Magione asked for Nurse Hilton by her first name, Joyce."

Mattias shook his head. "That's not enough. We need proof."

"Guess what else," Mae said. "The captain's sick, and we're getting a helicopter delivery of IV fluid because we're running short."

"A helicopter delivery!" Clinton said. "We've got to see that!"

"Let's go back to the cabin and get our cameras."

Back at the cabin Mae saw that there was a voice message on the phone. She punched in the code to retrieve the voice message. The message was from Dr. Reyes. "Mae, I wanted to let you know, your mother's sick. Now, neither one of us wants you to worry. We've moved her into one of the empty beds, and we're making her comfortable. Nurse Hilton is with her now. I called her in early to help. Your mom told me about your concerns with her, and I'm taking it very seriously. I've told Nurse Hilton she is not to go into the lab. But she's a fine nurse, Mae, and we really need her with your mom sick."

Mae called down to the infirmary and Dr. Reyes answered.

"Dr. Reyes, I'm coming right over."

Dr. Reyes said, "I'm sorry, Mae, but your mother gave firm instructions that you're not to come. She says to take a shower."

"I already did that," Mae said crossly. "She was already getting sick, wasn't she, when she sent me away. That's why she was acting so weird and trying to get me out of there."

"She's concerned for you," Dr. Reyes said. "Now I have to go. We're expecting the helicopter. If we can, I'm going to evacuate Mr. Magione."

Mae set down the phone with shaky hands. "My mom's sick," she said to Mattias. "First your sister, now my mom. We have to get these guys. Mattias, I want to read that article about Mrs. Magione."

Mattias shuffled his feet. "Um, about that. Someone cleaned the room and my printout got thrown out with the trash. And now the Internet's down again."

"Well, fix it!" Mae said crossly. "Use your Fix-it Stick or whatever it is and get me that article."

Mattias looked startled. "Sure. Um, I will. How did you know about—never mind. Look, I'll go work on it right now."

Clinton slapped his hands on the table and said, "Me, I'm going to go check on that helicopter delivery. Mae?"

Chapter 15

Helicopter Delivery and Hurricane Meals

Thursday

Spray whipped past as Mae hesitated at the door to the main deck. "This doesn't seem like a great idea."

"Oh, come on," Clinton said. "When are you ever going to see a helicopter land on a pitching deck, if not today?"

"I wish we had jackets," Mae said. She pushed on the door, but it took Clinton leaning on it too to get it open.

The wind was strangely warm and beat against them as they pulled themselves forward along the railing. They found a place where an alcove of the bridge gave them some protection. Forward, three crew members braced themselves around a circular marking on the deck. One of them wore a headset and seemed to be talking into it, but Mae couldn't hear him over the howling wind. Mae looked up but couldn't see any sign of a helicopter among the low gray clouds.

"We should at least put life jackets on," Mae said in a small voice.

"Yeah, you're right," Clinton said. "Stay here." He made his way back along the deck and returned in a couple of minutes with two orange life jackets hanging from one hand. They helped each other put the jackets on and cinch them tight. Then they heard the beating of helicopter rotors overhead.

"Out here where we can see," Clinton said. He led Mae out to the railing, and they held on.

A helicopter approached, flying about forty feet above the deck. It came close, hovered, and then swooped low. The wind caught it and it slid sideways, rose, and came in again. It seemed to be pitching up and down, but maybe that was the deck pitching. Mae felt her stomach lurch, and then her jaw clenched as the deck of the ship pitched up just as the chopper pitched down.

"Watch out!" someone cried, and the crew members threw themselves to the deck, as far from the landing site as possible.

But the chopper jerked up in time and swerved far out to sea. The man with the headphones talked rapidly and then turned to the officer next to him, shaking his head.

"They're deciding it's not safe to land," Clinton said.

"But what about Mr. Magione?" Mae said. "And what about the IV fluid?"

"I don't know," Clinton said. "Wait, look, he's coming back."

The helicopter approached again and hovered twenty feet above the deck. A door opened, and a cable descended, holding a large black rubber bag on the end.

"They're dropping it off," Clinton said. "Look at that."

The bag and cable swung in the wind as the chopper tried to hold steady above the slanting deck. Crew members backed out of the way of the swinging bag as it came lower. Clinton crept forward along the rail, and Mae followed him, shielding her eyes against the spray.

The man with the headset raised his arm. "Drop her. Now!" he shouted, and he let his arm fall. The cable let go, and the bag thudded heavily to the deck, falling open and spreading some of its contents over the circle. Just then, the ship pitched on a giant wave, and the black bag slid toward the side just forward of where Mae and Clinton clutched the rail.

"Hold my feet, Mae!" Clinton shouted. He launched himself full length to tackle the sliding bag. Mae grabbed for his feet. The bag and Clinton slid toward the side, and the bag tipped over the edge.

"Clinton, let go! Let go!" Mae shouted. She had hold of both his ankles and one of her legs wrapped through the railing, but the bag was drooping over the side now, pulling Clinton with it. Mae closed her eyes and pulled with all her might. The sound of crew members' running feet pounded on the deck.

Then suddenly Mae fell backward. Clinton had let the bag go. A crew member helped Mae up, and another dragged Clinton up beside her. Mr. Hammond stood in front of her, his face red with anger. "It is NOT SAFE up here. The two of you could have been killed. I should confine you both to quarters."

"But you were losing the IV fluid," Mae said. She was furious with Clinton for putting them both in danger, but she was just as furious at these stupid ship's officers who couldn't seem to get anything right.

"We saved quite a few bags," Mr. Hammond said, "and we'll take them to Dr. Reyes as soon as you clear the deck. IV bags are not worth two children's lives."

He grabbed them both by the collars of their life jackets and marched them to the door. He opened it and marched them inside. "Don't scare me like that," he said. "Here, give me your life jackets and go dry off. And remember, please, this ship does have a crew. We can take care of things."

"Oh, yeah," Clinton said as they slunk away down the hall. "They're taking care of things just great."

"That was crazy, Clinton," Mae said. "I thought you were going over."

Clinton nodded, his face serious. "I know. Thanks for holding on."

Mae took a hot shower and put on her warmest clothes, but she was still shivering as she walked up to the infirmary to check on her mother. Nurse Hilton stopped her at the infirmary entrance. "We're trying to keep visitors to a minimum," she said. "We're very busy here."

"Just let me see my mom for a moment," Mae said. "Two minutes, I promise."

Mae's mom was sleeping with her mouth open. She wore a hospital gown and her hair was matted. Mae patted her sleeping mother's shoulder. Under the bed lay a garbage bag, and when Mae pulled it out and opened it, she jerked her head back at the smell. It was her mother's uniform, and after a moment's hesitation, Mae rummaged through its pockets and came out with a key. She closed the bag and slid it back under the bed, and then she washed both her hands and the key with soap and hot water at the bedside sink. She said a soft goodbye to her sleeping mother and slipped out.

"Why are there dirty clothes under my mom's bed?" she asked Nurse Hilton.

Nurse Hilton pushed a strand of hair behind her ear. "The orderly will be here any moment to make a laundry run," she said. "We're so short-staffed." She looked as if she was about to cry.

"Well, then," Mae said. "We just have to make sure there are no more new cases, don't we, Nurse Hilton?"

Nurse Hilton put a hand to her throat as if she felt herself choking.

From outside in the hall, Mae quietly let herself into the lab and went to count the patient sample plates in the incubator. The numbers were the same as before. Mae left, letting the door lock behind her. What she really wanted to do now was go lie down and read a comic book or something, but it was almost time for the final session of the adult cooking contest. She called Mattias and agreed to meet him in the cooking studio. As for Clinton, the more she thought about how he'd almost dragged the two of them into the ocean with his stupid heroics, the less she felt like talking to him.

Mae slipped in next to Mattias. Clinton waved to her from Mattias' other side, but she ignored him and looked around the crowd instead. Julia and Jacques were there, wearing their *Cooking Genius* aprons. And sitting on the end of a row, wearing dark glasses and a Baltimore Orioles cap pulled down low, was someone who might be the disgraced Mr. Bouillon. Heinz stood on stage with two other contestants, each crouched behind a cooking station ready to begin. Nobody from the infirmary was here today.

"Today we welcome our new contestant, Heinz Merkel," Ms. Shires announced. "Like our young Cooking Geniuses yesterday, today's contestants are encouraged to use all the fancy equipment they can see to whip up a creative dish. The winning dish will be served at tonight's midnight buffet, and the winner will receive a five thousand dollar award. Now in honor of today's weather, our theme for today's contest is to prepare a Hurricane Special! You have an hour. Begin!"

The three chefs didn't hesitate. Immediately they grabbed bowls and began chopping and whipping ingredients. Mae forced herself to look away from the frenzy of preparation on stage and check around the room for anything suspicious. Mr. Bouillon had pulled out a pocket notebook and was making notes, lifting his head to check on what the chefs were doing and then scribbling with a stubby pencil. Either he was spying on their recipes or he was figuring out where to introduce the bacteria. Not good.

Then a door opened and Mrs. Magione shuffled in. She was wearing loafers instead of her usual heels, and her hair was uncombed. She pushed past several people and sat two rows ahead of Mae. "What a travesty," she said loudly to the person next to her. "When that criminal Bouillon was eliminated, they should have chosen from one of the eminent chefs aboard this ship. Instead they give the slot to one of their own. It's a fix, I tell you. That German guy of theirs, they've set him up to win. Mark my words. That Heinz will win even though his dish will be a disaster." Then Mrs. Magione shut her mouth and stared grimly at the stage.

The three chefs on stage worked with liquid nitrogen, the foam whipper, and the *sous vide* cooker. About forty minutes into the contest, a man in the audience pointed out Mr. Bouillon and started talking loudly about "Typhoid Bouillon." The television camera even swerved to focus on the restaurant owner in his dark glasses and baseball cap. Mr. Bouillon shoved his notebook in his pocket, pulled his hat down lower over his face, hunched his shoulders up to his ears, and slunk away.

"Stop!" Ms. Shires said twenty minutes later. "Now it's time for our judging. We're having a surprise feature today. Because one of our contestants is a member of our own staff, we're asking for some replacement judges to join us from the audience. Our first vote will come from a pair of judges, the winners of the *Cooking Genius* junior contest. Let's hear it for Jacques and Julia Revere of Delaware."

The audience clapped, and a pair of apron-clad but surprised-looking teenagers made their way down to crowd onto a single chair at the judges' table.

Clinton hissed and said softly, "That could have been us down there."

"Next," Ms. Shires announced, "we have a well-known restaurant owner." Two rows down, Mrs. Magione sat up and primped her hair. Ms. Shires continued, "Please welcome Thomas Elliott Uphaven of The Rooster's Crown in Aspen, Colorado." The crowd clapped again, as a tall, elegant man stood, leaned down to kiss the top of his wife's head, and walked down to the stage.

"Uh-oh, that makes him another suspect," Mae said.

"And for our final judge," Ms. Shires said, turning around to regard the audience with a smile, "we would like to invite Mrs. Marguerite O'Malley Magione, of the late Burgundy Bistro, to join us on stage."

Mrs. Magione stood and looked into the television camera. This is her moment, Mae thought. She must be deliriously happy.

Mrs. Magione spoke in a clear, loud voice. "I cannot allow my reputation to be muddied by association with this sorry ship's mediocre cuisine. This contest is rigged. You can be sure *I* won't be joining you at the midnight buffet, and I suspect that anyone who does will be sorry." With that, Ms. Magione pushed her way down the row of seated audience members and departed through the side door. Several members of the audience clapped when she left.

"Er, in that case," Ms. Shires said, "I think we'll have to return to one of our old reliable judges. Is our pastry chef here?"

The pastry chef, Sandrine Childs, wound her way down to sit at the table beside the other three judges. As soon as they had settled, Ms. Shires invited the competing chefs to come down and describe their concoctions.

"We will first have Yannis Papamichael, owner of the New Greek Taverna in Washington D.C., present and describe his dishes," Ms. Shires announced.

"I present to the esteemed judges my two Hurricane specials, the Frozen Chocolate Wind and the Liquid Nitrogen Orange and Stormy Sorbet," Mr. Papamichael said. "The Chocolate Wind was made using an emulsification technique and will feel light on your tongue."

The judges tasted the Frozen Chocolate Wind, and smiles broke out across the table. The young Cooking Geniuses cleaned their plate in a second.

"We could be the ones tasting that," Clinton said.

"Be quiet," Mae said.

Yannis Papamichael continued. "For the second dessert, I mixed fresh squeezed blood oranges with rum, an alcohol that does not normally freeze in your freezer. I used liquid nitrogen at negative 320 degrees Fahrenheit. It's cold enough to freeze the rum and the oranges together. It's a take on the classic dark and stormy drink." Mr. Papamichael smiled and spread his arms.

"Uh, we'll have the two young judges skip this one," Ms. Shires said as Julia and Jacques frowned. "I'll be happy to taste it, though," Ms. Shires added.

Mr. Uphaven, Ms. Childs, and Ms. Shires looked at each other and lifted spoons full of sorbet to their mouths. This time sounds of "yum" joined the smiles.

"Now let's have our next contestant come forward. Heinz Merkel!" Ms. Shires announced.

Heinz came forward with his own platter of two desserts.

"I have created an Apple Caviar with Banana Sea Foam and a Seaweed Miso Sponge Cake." Heinz said. "The caviar was created using a spherification process and the sea foam was made using the culinary whipper. For the sponge cake I used both nitrous oxide and a microwave oven."

All of a sudden, Mae jumped to her feet. "That's it!" Mae cried. "We have them!"

"Have what?" Clinton said. "Heinz's recipes?"

"No," Mae said. "Out in the corridor." She jumped off her seat, and the boys followed.

"We're missing the last contestant," Clinton complained.

"Tough," Mae said. "Didn't you hear Ms. Shires call Mrs. Magione by her full name?

"What are you talking about?" Clinton asked.

"It took a minute to sink in, but she said it right out loud. Mrs. Marguerite O'Malley Magione. O'Malley, O'Malley, don't you see?"

Chapter 16

U.S. Army Research Center and Bio-Detection

Natick, Massachusetts, Thursday

"Wait a minute," Clinton said. "Nurse Hilton's diploma said Joyce O'Malley."

"Joyce O'Malley and Marguerite O'Malley," Mae said. "They're related. It's the connection we were looking for."

Clinton slapped his thigh. "You're right, we have them," he said. "We're going to the captain right now."

"The captain's in the infirmary," Mae reminded him. "It's more like we have to go to Mr. Hammond."

Clinton grimaced. "Er, we're not exactly on his good list right now. I don't think he'll listen to us without proof."

"Maybe the villains won't try it again," Mattias suggested. "Maybe two attacks are enough."

"But you heard her," Mae said. "Mrs. Magione said Heinz's dish would be a disaster and anyone who went to the midnight buffet would be sorry."

"I don't think we have to worry," Clinton said. "Heinz won't win, not with a dessert cake made out of seaweed."

Before Mae could answer that even ice cream was made of seaweed, the studio doors flew open and the audience flowed out, laughing and talking. Apparently Heinz had won by unanimous vote for his Apple Caviar with Banana Sea Foam and Seaweed Miso Sponge Cake. Clinton pushed through the crowd to congratulate him. He leaned close to Heinz's ear and said, "Listen, I have to talk to you. We don't want your dish getting infected like Mr. Bouillon's. Meet you by the pool in ten minutes."

Clinton made his way back to where Mattias and Mae were waiting. "Look, I think we can guard Heinz's dish really carefully, but I don't know how we can catch Hilton and Magione, or should I call them the O'Malley girls, red-handed."

"Me neither," Mattias said. "Maybe just keep trailing them. Listen, I'll go back to my room and try to pull up that article and anything I can find about Nurse Hilton. You two do what you can. Meet you at dinner. What say the Taco Bar at six?" He walked away into the crowd.

"Now what?" Clinton said. "Don't look at me that way, Mae. I know I was an idiot before. It's just—the X-PA sometimes makes me feel a little too invulnerable, you know? It's taken us so many places." He pulled it out of his pocket and gazed at it. "I mean, it's a good friend, but—Hey! Look at this. There's a new destination."

"Let's see," Mae said, pulling on his wrist. She read, *"Kelsey Sonoma, biosensors, U.S. Army Research Center, Natick, Massachusetts.* That's not far from home."

"Shall we do it?" Clinton asked. "It won't take any time."

"I guess so," Mae said, and Clinton made the loop.

They stood on a lawn in the weak spring sunlight. They were inside a security fence, and a sign read, "U.S. Army Research Center." Several brick buildings stood scattered around, and they walked toward the closest one. A soldier with a gun slung over one shoulder approached them.

"Cool gun," Clinton said, and Mae elbowed him.

"How did you get separated from your school group?" the soldier asked. "Hurry up. They're in this building."

"Is Dr. Kelsey Sonoma in this building?" Mae asked.

"She's probably just finished her presentation on the bacterial sensor. Yes, look, here comes your group now. Stay with them," the soldier said sternly, and then he went back outside to take up his post.

Kids their own age passed by, giving Clinton and Mae in their shorts and sandals a curious look. "What do you say?" Clinton asked Mae. "Do we go where they came from and throw ourselves on Dr. Sonoma's mercy?"

Mae nodded.

They pushed through the door the class had just come through. A young woman with long dark hair in a ponytail stood holding what looked like a TV remote control.

"Excuse me, are you Dr. Sonoma?" Clinton asked.

"Yes, I am. Are you lost? The group went that way."

"We're not lost and we're not part of the group," Mae blurted. "We came just to see you. Is it true you have a way to sense bacteria?"

Dr. Sonoma waved the object that looked like a TV remote control. "We're working on one. You wave this over the food and wait a few seconds. A green light will turn on if there are no dangerous microbes on the food."

"And what if there are microbes?" Clinton asked.

"It lights up red," Dr. Sonoma said with a smile.

"How does it work?" Mae asked.

"A small puff of air from the sensor releases any microbes from the surface and catches them in the sample chamber. Antibodies with fluorescent tags have already been injected into the sample chamber. If there are any bacteria, the antibodies latch onto them. After few seconds, a light detector picks up any light from the antibodies." Dr. Sonoma said.

"That's amazing. Why not sell it to everyone?" Clinton asked.

"Well, it doesn't quite work all the time." Dr. Sonoma said. "This is still a research project. So far we've only set it up for E. coli O:157. Have you heard of that?"

"Sure," Clinton said. "Toxigenic E. coli, one of the most common causes of traveler's diarrhea."

"Wow." Dr. Sonoma looked impressed. "The sensor I have in my hand is only a prototype. It's not quite working the way I want. Actually, this particular approach may never work reliably. But that is part of R&D and making advances."

"What's R&D?" Clinton asked.

"Research and development." Dr. Sonoma said. "We need scientists and engineers to work together, having wild ideas and then tinkering away on those ideas to make new tools and materials." She smiled. "It's a blast. Maybe both of you will do R&D and create new technologies in the future."

"Well, right now, we're trying to solve a case of food poisoning on a ship…in a book we're reading at school." Clinton said.

"Food-borne illnesses on ships can spread quickly," Dr. Sonoma said. "I've actually done some historical research about how advances in food technologies have increased how far ships can travel. Think about it. If you don't have safe food to last you even a few days, then you can only go a few hundred miles. But to cross an ocean under wind power, you need safe food for weeks and months. In the 1700s, the big problem was not enough of the right kind of food. Sailors died of scurvy, with their teeth falling out and wounds not healing for lack of vitamin C. Then the English navy figured out citrus fruit would prevent scurvy, and they added lemons and limes to the sailors' grog. That's why English sailors were called Limeys."

"Well, cruise ships have lots of delicious food," Clinton said.

"That's right. They load up with tons of food and water, and they have canning and freezing and refrigeration to preserve it. Submarines too. They can stay submerged for weeks if they have to."

"But there's that pesky problem of contamination and food-borne illness," Clinton said.

Dr. Sonoma nodded. "There are new technologies other than mine that are being developed to scan for dangerous microbes," she said. "For now, we're stuck with incubators to grow enough microbes from a sample so that we can detect their presence."

Mae said, "But an incubator could also be used to grow bacteria to poison food, couldn't it?"

"Certainly, but that would be biowarfare," Dr. Sonoma said. "To have a major effect on a country it would have to happen at an industrial scale, infecting lots and lots of food at the same time. It's a serious concern and one the Army is working on."

"I don't suppose you have a bacterial sensor we could borrow for a few minutes," Clinton said. "We'd bring it right back."

Dr. Sonoma shook her head.

Clinton said, "Well, thanks for your time. We'll find our own way out."

As they walked toward the front door, Mae said, "Well, that was interesting, but not really any use. They don't even have one that really works yet."

"Mrs. Magione doesn't know that," Clinton said. "Let's find Mattias. I have a plan."

Chapter 17

Midnight Buffet

Thursday to Friday

Clinton trailed Mrs. Magione for the rest of the afternoon. To his surprise, she didn't go to visit her husband in the infirmary again. Instead, she spent a long time playing bingo. There weren't a lot of kids in the bingo room—actually, there weren't any— so Clinton sat up front ordering lemonade after lemonade. His chance came when Mrs. Magione took a break from her winnings and came up to order a Bloody Mary.

"I couldn't believe Heinz would do that, Mrs. Magione," Clinton said loudly. "I mean, I know you weren't exactly polite about him, but to do what he did!"

"What, what?" Mrs. Magione asked, looking around herself as if someone had pinned a "Kick Me" sign to her back.

"I mean bringing up that old story about botulism," Clinton said even more loudly. "Telling everyone how your restaurant got closed down after two people were paralyzed. I mean, that's the past, isn't it! More than a year ago!"

Several bingo players looked their way, and a buzz of conversation started as players put their heads together. The buzz spread so quickly that soon the bingo caller stopped, listening with eyebrows raised to the pair of ladies in front of him.

Mrs. Magione stood up. "He said that? That's slander. I'll sue. I'm going to have a word with the captain."

"Don't you know?" Clinton asked sweetly. "The captain's in the infirmary with a food-borne illness."

"Well I...I..." Mrs. Magione sputtered. Then, seemingly at a loss for any more threats, she headed for the door and went to the nearest phone in the hallway. Clinton trailed her that far, but he didn't dare get too close. He saw her put the phone to her ear and heard her say, "Joyce? Joyce?"

Clinton waited for Mrs. Magione to finish her call and leave. Then he picked up the phone to call Mae in the lab. "I baited the trap," he said. "She called someone named Joyce. I think we're on."

"Are you going to keep following her?" Mae asked.

"If I can find her. First I'm going to go warn Heinz not to let that dessert out of his sight. He's got to bring it to the midnight buffet all by himself. See you soon."

Mae went to the door of the lab and signaled to Dr. Reyes. He came in, looking weary and unenthusiastic.

"Did Nurse Hilton just get a phone call?" she asked.

"Yes, she did," Dr. Reyes said. "What of it? Staff are allowed to take phone calls on duty, especially when they're working double shifts the way she is."

"Please listen," Mae said. "I know you don't want to think one of your staff is involved in this outbreak, but we have pretty good evidence she is. If you and I both leave for a few minutes, I bet you five dollars Joyce Hilton is going to take a sample from this incubator."

"All right, Mae," Dr. Reyes said. "You've been a great help so far, so I'll be a good sport and take your bet." He sighed and ran a hand over his beautifully groomed hair. "Besides, I could use a break. I'll tell her I'm getting a sandwich." He exited the lab room, and Mae heard his level voice in the infirmary.

A couple of minutes later, Mae stuck her head into the infirmary too. "Nurse Hilton?" she called. The nurse, her eyes red, stepped out from behind a curtain. "Will you say goodbye to my mom?" Mae asked. "One of my friends just called, and we're going swimming."

Then she walked out the infirmary door, swinging her book and trying very hard to look lighthearted, like someone without a sick mother or a mystery to solve.

Mae waited around the corner, forcing herself to be patient, until Dr. Reyes returned. "Well?" he said, raising his eyebrows as he strode down the hall.

"Distract her," Mae said. "I'm going in to count the plates."

Mae waited thirty more seconds and then walked down the hall to the lab. She used her mother's key to let herself in. Heart pounding, she opened the incubator. She counted the plates twice. Two missing. She checked her records. The two missing plates were growing two different bacterial samples, *B. cereus* and *Campylobacter.*

Mae sat at the desk. In spite of everything, she had a hard time believing a nurse, even a nurse related to a crazy angry restaurant lady, would purposely make people sick.

In a couple of minutes, Dr. Reyes came into the lab and closed the door. "Well?" he said again.

"You owe me five dollars," Mae said. Instead of feeling happy, she felt like crying. "She took two plates, one of each kind of bacteria."

"I'll call security," Dr. Reyes said.

"No, not yet," Mae said. "She'll just say she wanted to check them or something."

Dr. Reyes looked relieved. "Maybe she just did want to check them. Maybe she was about to put them back when a patient rang a bell."

"Maybe," Mae said. "But there's one more step that will help us be sure. I need you to bring Nurse Hilton to the midnight buffet. You need to be there right at the start."

"I can't do that," Dr. Reyes said. "Who will be watching the patients?"

"Doesn't the crew have some sort of first aid officer?" Mae said. "We'll only need about ten minutes. If nothing happens by then, you can go back."

Dr. Reyes considered. "You're very persuasive," he said at last. "How does your mother manage you?"

Clinton and Mae stood outside the buffet, waiting for Mattias to show up. Clinton showed Mae his doctored cell phone, wrapped in shiny metallic tape and with what looked like a tiny radar attached.

"Just don't let them look too close," Mae said.

"I just hope I can keep from laughing," Clinton answered.

Mattias turned the corner, and beside him, looking exhausted but alert, walked Riley. Mae went to hug her, but Riley stepped back. "Dr. Reyes let me out for an hour, but I had to promise not to touch anybody," she said.

"I've told her everything," Mattias said. "She has some important evidence."

"There was an argument," Riley said. "I woke up because the two of them were trying to talk quietly but their voices kept going up."

"Who?" Mae asked.

"The nurse and the restaurant lady. The one with the sick husband."

Mattias encouraged her. "You mean Mrs. Magione." To the others he said, "She's still kind of out of it."

"Yes, Mrs. Magione," Riley said. "I'd know that voice anywhere. And Nurse Hilton kept saying, 'No, I don't want to anymore, people are really sick, you can't have them.' And Mrs. Magione said, 'Who paid for your nursing school? What would your mother say about you abandoning me now?'"

"So Mrs. Magione is Joyce Hilton's aunt," Mae said.

Riley nodded her head. "And then all of a sudden Nurse Hilton shouted, 'No, you can't take that! It's mine, it's mine!' So I jumped out of bed and stuck my head through the curtains and asked her what was going on. She was standing there holding a purse, and she looked at me and said, 'Someone accidentally switched purses with me.'"

"Oh, wow," Mae said. "She hid the plates in her purse, and now Mrs. Magione has them."

"And now we will have Mrs. Magione," Clinton said. "Stations, everybody."

A cart came rolling up the corridor. The steward who was rolling it winked at Mattias.

"Any help from Mrs. Magione?" Mattias asked.

The steward shook his head.

"Good," Clinton said.

Another cart came, and another. The answer to Mattias' question was always the same.

"Maybe they chickened out," Mattias said.

"I don't think so," Clinton said. "Mrs. Magione was really mad. If we're right, she'll attack right here at the buffet."

Heinz rolled up the last cart, taking big breaths as if he was an opera singer about to go on stage for his big scene. He stopped right beside Clinton. "Guess who wanted to apologize and help me with my cart?" he said.

"No!" Mae said. "You didn't let her, I hope?"

Heinz shook his head, grinning, and pushed his cart through the double doors.

People began to gather around them outside the doors, and Mattias wandered off to talk to Mr. Hammond. At the stroke of midnight, the doors opened. Mae waited outside with Riley as the boys went in to guard the buffet table, with Clinton standing at the dessert end next to Heinz. At two minutes past midnight, Dr. Reyes entered, snazzy in a suit, with Nurse Joyce Hilton on his arm. Nurse Hilton wore a red dress and pearls, and Mae felt a stab of jealousy on her mother's behalf. Wow, how did that happen? At first she'd hated it when Dr. Reyes paid attention to her mother. Now she hated it when he paid attention to someone else. She gave the couple a wobbly smile, and she and Riley followed them into the dining room.

Five minutes later, Mrs. Magione arrived. She wore a sequined dress and stiletto heels, and she held a glass of alcohol in her hands. As soon as Mae saw her, she ran around the end of the buffet line to stand between Clinton and Heinz, and she fixed her eyes on Mrs. Magione. Mrs. Magione carried a large canvas purse that did not match her dress. The purse hung partway open, and Mrs. Magione swayed a little as she walked. She pushed right through to the front of the buffet line, and when she came to Heinz's Apple Caviar she used the serving spoon to dish a spoonful of Banana Sea Foam right into her mouth. She pulled up and looked surprised. "Oh dear, I shouldn't have done that, should I?" she asked brightly. As everyone turned to look, she spilled her drink down her front. Starting back, she dropped her glass onto the floor, where it shattered. The other guests jumped. Then the server next to Heinz handed a napkin across to Mrs. Magione, and the man behind her in line hastened to lead her to a table. Riley took a chair across the table from her.

Mrs. Magione sank into her chair and burst into tears. "My Bernie," she wept. "My Bernie's so sick."

"Oh, man," Clinton said. "We blew it. She's too drunk to try anything."

"No," Mae said. "Wait. It was like a magic trick."

"What do you mean?"

"Did you watch her hands after she dropped the glass? You didn't, did you? No one did. They all looked at the shattered glass. Now she has a whole room full of people who can swear she didn't put anything in the food. But I saw her kind of brush her hand over it."

"Oh," Clinton said. "Mae, you're really smart."

"You have to do your thing," Mae said. "Go on."

Clinton gulped and swaggered to the front of the buffet table. Class clown, he told himself. You can do it. Play the class clown. "Wait, folks," he said with a drawl. "I should have brought this out before. My engineer dad helped me. This little doohickey won me grand prize at the science fair." He held up his doctored cell phone and turned all the way around so everybody could see it, but all in a blur. "It's a bacterial sensor for food safety. See, this little puff of air raises any bacteria from the food surface, and the fluorescent antibodies bound to nano tubes inside give off light if bacteria bind to them..." As he talked, he waved the cell phone over the surface of the foods all down the buffet line. "Now, it isn't perfect yet, and it isn't as sensitive as I'd like, but one thing is sure, if the tone sounds, you can be sure there's—Oh, wow, look at that!" A tone sounded from the phone as Clinton halted over Heinz's Apple Caviar. "Red light. Oh, I can't believe it, it's happening again. This food isn't safe!"

Voices rose in doubt and argument as Clinton trotted over to the chair where Mrs. Magione sat weeping. Dr. Reyes stepped closer too, drawing Joyce Hilton with him.

"Mrs. Magione, you ate some of that," Clinton said in a voice of deep concern. "Here, stick out your tongue and let me check it. You don't want to? I understand, Mrs. O'Malley, but..."

Mrs. Magione's head jerked at the sound of her maiden name.

"But wait!" Clinton said in his loudest, most surprised voice. "I'm getting a strong reading right here from your pocket, or is it your purse?" He darted his other hand out and knocked Mrs. Magione's purse off the table and onto the floor.

Both Mrs. Magione and Nurse Hilton threw themselves to the floor, reaching for the purse. Then, with a crafty look on her face, Mrs. Magione pulled back. "It's not my purse," she said. "You see. It's hers, not mine."

Clinton turned to Nurse Hilton. "Joyce O'Malley," he said in a voice of doom, "What's in that purse?"

Nurse Hilton gave a little scream and seemed to faint into Dr. Reyes' arms. He was having none of it. He looped his foot around a chair leg, pulled it forward, and holding his nurse by her upper arms, sat her down. "If you feel faint, put your head between your knees," he instructed her. "But first, tell me what you did with those two plates of bacteria you stole from the incubator this afternoon."

Nurse Hilton, like Mrs. Magione before her, dissolved into tears. "I didn't want to," she said. "She's my aunt. She bullied me. I didn't want to do it."

Mr. Hammond put a hand on Mrs. Magione's shoulder and nodded to another ship's officer, who took hold of Nurse Hilton's arm. "We're going to have to search your cabins," Mr. Hammond said. "Ladies and gentlemen, this midnight buffet is canceled. You will find tacos at the Taco Bar and burgers at the poolside."

Amid the uproar, four crew members led the two women away. Clinton came over to Mae. "I can't believe those two fell for it," he said in a shaky voice.

Dr. Reyes spoke up beside them. "Guilt will do that to a person," he said.

"Speaking of guilt," Mae said, "you snuck out of that laboratory without giving me my five dollars."

Dr. Reyes' mouth fell open and he patted his pockets. "Oh, dear. Mae, I'm sorry, I don't have it with me. If you come up to the infirmary, I know I have some up there."

"We'll come along," Mattias said. "Riley should get back to the infirmary anyway."

"I wanted to hug Mrs. Magione," Riley said. "I wanted to wrap my arms around her and slobber all over her, hoping I'm still infectious."

"It's better not to do that," Dr. Reyes said. "We should always try to imitate those who are better than us, not those who are worse. Come on, kids."

As they walked along the corridors to the infirmary, Mae said, "I suppose Mrs. Magione is already being punished. She seems really upset about her husband. He must have eaten some of the wrong food without her knowing."

"I wish I was sure of that," Dr. Reyes said. "A sick husband whose life is put in danger by food poisoning—what could be better for a lawsuit? She was all set to make money from him. And if he died, well, I hate to say it, but I'd sure be interested in how much life insurance he carries." He ground his teeth. "I wonder how she corrupted my nurse."

When they reached the infirmary, Dr. Reyes rummaged in the pocket of his white coat and came up with a crumpled five-dollar bill. As he handed it to Mae, his phone rang, and he said things like "Hmm" and "You don't say" until he hung up. He told the four teenagers, "That was Mr. Hammond. That purse was full of cotton swabs with wet gunk on their ends, and in Nurse Hilton's room they found both a number of bacterial plates and a medicine cabinet full of antibiotics. It seems she's been medicating herself to fight off all the bacteria she was handling." He shook his head. "Mr. Hammond's sending a steward up with the evidence for me to stain and culture."

Mattias offered to help Riley back into bed while Mae headed in to say good night to her mom. She expected to find her asleep, but instead her mom turned over and gazed at her

174

daughter through half-open eyes. "Hello, sweetie," she said. "Isn't it bedtime? What's all that jabber I hear out there?"

"We found them, Mom." Mae stepped close and took hold of her mother's hand. "We found the people infecting the food. They were doing it on purpose. It was Nurse Hilton and Mrs. Magione, Mom."

"Imagine that," Mae's mom said softly. She drew her hand away, turned over and snuggled into her pillow, and said in a voice thick with sleep, "Remember to wash your hands."

All at once, Mae felt very tired. She went back out to where Dr. Reyes and Clinton were waiting. "Do you need some help with the evidence?" she asked Dr. Reyes.

"I can handle it," Dr. Reyes said with a smile. "Child labor's illegal, you know. Especially after midnight. I have a crew member to help watch the patients, and I'll sleep on the couch. Don't worry. I've done it before."

Mae and Clinton left the infirmary. As they rounded a corner, a teenaged girl in pink and green stepped from the shadows. Clinton handed her the X-PA. "Good night, Selectra," he said. "We're too tired to talk."

Selectra Volt stood aside to let them pass.

Clinton spoke his final words over his shoulder. "And say hi to Mattias and Riley."

ABOUT THE AUTHORS

Peter Wong has been involved with Science, Technology, Engineering, and Math (STEM) research and education throughout his career as a former professor at Tufts University (Medford, MA), curriculum developer at the Museum of Science (Boston, MA), founder of K2 Enrichment After School Program (Newton, MA), former board member of the Massachusetts State Science and Engineering Fair, and now as co-founder of Tumblehome Learning (Boston, MA). Through his work with Tumblehome Learning, he is developing products that can inspire children to learn STEM through exciting adventure books, hands-on activities, and new technologies. He has a passion to make STEM a part of everyone's lives whether in school, after school, at home, or outside at play.

Peter was born and raised in Boston, Massachusetts. His primary and secondary education were in the Boston Public School system, and he graduated from Boston Latin School. He studied Mechanical Engineering at Tufts University and received his bachelor, master, and doctoral degrees from there. Peter continues his lifelong learning in technical topics (e.g., thermal processing, comparative biomechanics, biomedical devices, and nanotechnology) and educational areas (e.g., STEM education, professional development for teachers, and informal science education). He enjoys cooking classic dishes and modern cuisines using the latest techniques and technologies (e.g., sous vide, culinary whipper, and liquid nitrogen).

Pendred Noyce is a physician, educator, mother of five, and children's author. She is a trustee of the Noyce Foundation, which supports efforts to improve K-12 math and science learning. Penny is also the author of the award-winning Lexicon Adventure series published by Scarletta Press.

G.A.S. SERIES

Clinton and Mae's Missions:

The Desperate Case of the Diamond Chip
The Vicious Case of the Viral Vaccine
The Baffling Case of the Battered Brain
The Perilous Case of the Zombie Potion
The Contaminated Case of the
Cooking Contest

Anita and Benson's Missions:

The Furious Case of the Fraudulent Fossil
The Harrowing Case of the Hackensack
Hacker
The Confounding Case of the Climate Crisis

Ella and Shomari's Mission:

The Cryptic Case of the Coded Fair

... and more G.A.S. adventures on the way!

JOIN TODAY!
THE GALACTIC ACADEMY OF SCIENCE
NEEDS YOU!

Buy more Galactic Academy of Science titles at Tumblehomelearning.com and retail outlets throughout the world. Other titles include: "*The Desperate Case of the Diamond Chip*", "*The Furious Case of the Fraudulent Fossil*", "*The Vicious Case of the Viral Vaccine*", "*The Harrowing Case of the Hackensack Hacker*", "*The Baffling Case of the Battered Brain*", "*The Cryptic Case of the Coded Fair*", "*The Perilous Case of the Zombie Potion*", "*The Confounding Case of the Climate Crisis*" and more.
There's a subject of scientific interest for everybody!

The Galactic Academy of Science (G.A.S.)
Defending the integrity of science through the ages